Marrying for Love

Superstitious Brides #1

A humorous contemporary romance novella by

Susan Ann Wall

MARRYING FOR LOVE

ISBN: 978-1-941852-05-7

Cover Images:
Foreground: © Katherine Elizabeth Photography
Design Heart of Jupiter Publishing

Edited by Mary Ann Jock

This is a work of fiction. Names, characters, places, and incidents are a creation from the author's imagination or are used fictitiously.

Dedication

For Jill F, whose bravery and positive spirit is a daily inspiration! Keep fighting!

~~

Susan Ann Wall

Chapter 1

WHEN THE RAP MUSIC MORPHED into screaming lyrics, Jill Butler screamed right along. The rickety old ladder on which she stood shook in rhythm with the music's beat, giving her heart a much-needed jolt. She'd been running on a sort of cathartic auto-pilot since arriving in Lilac Ridge nearly a week ago, breaking her vow to never return to the northern New Hampshire town she'd once called home.

Regret over that vow made her chest ache as she balanced precariously on the ladder. If Jill had been able to let go of the past, maybe she could have seen her Great Aunt Sissy one last time before she died.

As the screaming petered out and the rap lyrics started again, Jill focused on the task at hand. The light fixture dangling in front of her represented the last inches of this house that had not received a thorough cleaning. It was day four of scrubbing down Sissy's old farmhouse and Jill was determined to sleep in a bed tonight instead of on her friend's couch. To do that, she had to eradicate all evidence of the cats who had taken up residence in the house. Jill had been off-balance since arriving in the town where she'd grown up and this endeavor was testing her limits, even before she'd started screaming.

1

The prescription allergy meds she took religiously were no match for a decade's worth of dust and dander as it tickled her nose. Jill held out her free arm in an attempt to balance as she reached for the fixture. Her exhibition was worthy of a circus performer and she figured if she couldn't keep Sissy's animal rescue afloat, she had options under the big top.

In fact, the circus seemed like a better option than making a life in the small town that held the ghosts of her past.

"Let it go, Jilly," she preached, and resumed singing, or wailing, since she sounded more like a cat in heat than a gifted musician. Life had to keep moving forward, she reminded herself. It was the only way to survive.

Jill sprayed the fixture again and leaned down to put the bottle on top of the ladder. The fixture liked to swing, requiring an extra hand to hold it steady. She climbed onto the top wrung, confident she could reach the shade without having to move the ladder. Pinching the shade between two fingers, Jill swiped the towel across the surface with her other hand. She was just about done when her cat allergy fully kicked in. The singing was replaced with a sneeze she couldn't hold back, sending the ladder toppling over.

That's when she realized she had no circus skills at all, and damn if this wasn't the worst time to discover that ineptitude.

As she choked on her heart, Jill bellowed out a string of colorful curses and closed her eyes, bracing for the hard landing on the kitchen floor.

When she came to an abrupt stop, there was no loud thud, no crunching of bones, no searing pain radiating through her body. No, there was just a warmth, across her back, under her knees, and across her cheek. She opened her eyes, nearly passing out when she met the piercing blue gaze of the man who caught her.

It may have been fifteen years since she'd last looked into them, but she would know those eyes anywhere.

"Jill," he whispered and her entire body turned to goo. Not the gross kind, but the pliable, needy, very hot kind.

"Austin," she whispered back before coming to her senses. Jill cleared her throat, "Austin Hale," she snarled, squirming in his arms in an attempt to loosen his hold on her.

He set her on the floor, not letting go. She stepped out of his hold, spreading her feet to steady herself. Steady was a relative term since she'd already been off-balance before the decrepit ladder doomed her. Smashing onto the floor would have been a safer alternative than landing in Austin's arms.

While she may be able to stand upright without assistance, her heart pounded like the hooves of a wild mare trying to escape the affection of an even wilder stallion.

"I wasn't expecting to find you here," Austin said, he too clearing his throat and pulling Jill's thoughts from the wild. "Why are you, uh," he turned, glancing at the stack of boxes in the mudroom before looking back at her. "Do you live here?"

The boxes were labeled with the contents and the room to which they belonged. Suitcases also occupied the space, the contents spilling out because Jill didn't want to put anything in the house until she'd eradicated the smell and allergens.

"No, yes, I mean," Jill took a deep breath. This was a disaster. As a project manager for a software company, she'd been able to handle the unexpected because that was the norm in her job. Projects went awry. It was something she'd come to expect.

Seeing Austin Hale standing in her aunt's – well, now Jill's – kitchen wasn't something she'd ever considered, let alone planned for. Had it been on her radar, she wouldn't be wearing a rag of a white t-shirt, ratty old cut-offs, and wreaking of cat urine, sweat, and industrial strength cleaner.

"Yes, I live here. Now, anyway. Since a week ago." Jill took another breath and decided to stick with the facts. "Sissy died." There was no point sugar-coating it. Her favorite aunt had died a couple weeks ago, not telling Jill she had stage four pancreatic cancer. Great Aunt Cecilia, having no children of her own, had left everything, including ten acres of land, the old farmhouse, and an animal rescue, to Jill.

"Oh, Jill, damn. I'm so sorry. I didn't know."

Austin's sympathy had Jill's heart plunging into her stomach. Even as a kid, he'd loved her aunt. Everyone had. Sissy was quirky but wise and she believed in love, perseverance, and forgiveness.

Jill had worked hard to be like her aunt. When it came to Austin Hale, however, love had failed, perseverance came in the form of staying away from him, and forgiveness was far beyond Jill's grasp.

"Why are you here?" she snapped, catching her breath. There was no time to dwell on Sissy's death or Austin's betrayal. There was only her to-do list and Austin was standing in the way of that.

"I moved home," he said and just like that her heart lodged back in her throat.

"No," she choked out, trying to pull something out of the vault of her crisis management skills. God, it sounded like she was horrified by his declaration – which, of course, she was. She'd come back to Lilac Ridge knowing Austin was an ocean away.

Austin laughed. "Is it really that horrible?"

Shaking words back into her scattered brain, Jill planted her hands on her hips. "No, I meant, why are you standing in my kitchen?"

"Oh, I, uh,"

The corner of Jill's lip started to lift at Austin's stammering, thrilled she wasn't the only one affected by this unexpected meeting. She steadied her amusement, crossing her arms to keep too much emotion from escaping.

"I need a dog. Want a dog. I want to adopt a dog. The sign at the Barn said to come to the house."

Her heart softened just a little, but before it got too mushy, Jill pulled in another stern breath. "We have an extensive adoption process," she half lied. "You'll have to fill out an application and we'll schedule a home visit and we'll need references. When all that is done, if you're approved, you can adopt a dog."

"Jilly," he sighed.

4

"It's Jill," she corrected, not willing to let him have any of the allowances he'd had when they were kids. "That's our process. I'm not going to make exceptions just because of your family name."

"You know I don't give a shit about my family name," he barked.

Jill coughed out a humorless laugh before swallowing the urge to tear him a new one while reminding him his family name was the reason he'd crushed her heart so long ago.

Crossing her arms, she steeled herself as best she could. "You're a Hale. Your name is everything and don't even try to deny it. If you want a dog from this rescue, you'll have to go through the same process as everyone else."

"Fine," he said, that soft affection he'd shown earlier now replaced with an air of annoyance that made Jill smile. "Give me an application."

Jill washed her hands, taking her sweet time because it was fun to make Austin wait. He gave no indication he was in a hurry, but the Hales always had someplace to be, some old hotel to buy up for measly pennies before turning it into some glorious five star resort that catered to the world's wealthiest tycoons.

Her turtle pace had nothing to do with keeping the man close enough to feel the heat and energy resonating from his very fine body.

Because it had been way too long since Jill had enjoyed the heat from a man, and she might just be on the wrong side of desperate. Even though she wanted to steal Austin's heat and energy, she wasn't about to let him be the man who scratched the very obvious itch she had going on.

Jill might be desperate, but she wasn't so desperate as to sell her soul to the devil himself.

As she dried her hands, memories of the boy who she loved before he turned into his father filled her heart.

Austin hadn't been drop-dead gorgeous as a kid. When he'd first started hanging around the Barn, he was a little overweight, a lot clumsy, and completely insecure. Jill had liked him because he worked hard and loved the animals. They'd become friends, the best of friends, before puberty blessed Austin with a transformation you only think ever happens in the movies. One day he showed up at the Barn to walk and feed the dogs with Jill and he'd erupted into a young man with toned muscles on a rugged frame, a light shadow of bristly facial hair, and piercing blue eyes that spoke of one thing.

Desire.

It had echoed all the way through Jill's body, making her forget her thoughts and lose words mid-sentence. Puberty had been a miracle, and lucky for Jill, Austin only had eyes for her.

Her luck had run out though, and Austin had tossed their friendship and love aside for his family. Jill hadn't just lost her heart in the process, she'd lost everything.

She tossed the towel aside in an effort to toss away those memories of long ago. With Austin's gaze burning a hole through her, she went to the makeshift desk in the corner and printed an application.

Jill looked at the clock and realized she only had minutes before she and Austin wouldn't be alone. She needed to get him out of there. "You can take this home and fill it out. Drop it by later in the week. Or just mail it." Mailing would be better, then she wouldn't have to see him again and maybe it would get lost.

"Nana said you have a golden retriever, Buttercup," he said as he took the application. "I'm willing to put a deposit on her while we go through the formalities."

"Buttercup's been adopted," Jill said. It was sort of the truth.

"Can I see what else you have for dogs?" he asked, his voice softening.

She glanced at the clock again. "I'm in the middle of something," she lied again, wishing he'd take the hint and leave. "We should get the paperwork processed first."

"The paperwork will be a waste of time if you don't have a dog I want."

"Sometimes the dog chooses you," she reminded him, which was why Buttercup wasn't available.

"I think you're trying to get rid of me," he smirked before glancing at the clock behind him that had always been there, even when they were kids. "You expecting someone?"

"As a matter of fact, I am. Take the application, send it back whenever. We'll be in touch."

She shimmied him toward the mudroom door at the back of the house and no sooner closed it than Buttercup came tearing through the house from the front door. Jill turned the lock and watched Austin get in his shiny black truck. Before he rolled away, he looked up at her, that spark she remembered flashing in his eyes.

When he drove off, she released her breath, not even realizing she'd been holding it.

"Who was that?" Eric asked. She turned to find her son leaning across the long kitchen counter, digging into a bag of potato chips. He stuffed his face with one hand and fed Buttercup with the other.

Jill could lie, tell him it was no one, but Austin being in Lilac Ridge changed everything. Jill couldn't pretend otherwise and she wouldn't lie to her son. "That was Austin Hale."

Eric's eyes widened to the size of the moon. "What? I thought he was in France?"

Me too, Jill thought. Had she known Austin was here in Lilac Ridge, she might not have come. She could have hired someone to home all the animals and then put the property up for sale. But Eric had wanted to come, to have a life that offered something different than the city.

As her son stared at her, waiting for an answer, Jill shrugged and said, "He told me he moved back."

Jill nearly cringed as hope filled Eric's blue eyes. "Moved back? Really?"

She shrugged again as if it was no big deal. "That's what he told me."

"So what did he want?" Eric asked, too much hope in his voice.

7

"He wants to adopt a dog," she chuckled because the humor of this whole situation was too potent to ignore.

Eric didn't laugh. A range of emotions crossed her young teen's face. Hope was replaced with fear, though she didn't know if it was fear for himself or fear for her.

"I'm not going to let him hurt you, Mom," Eric said. He was the most empathetic person she'd ever known and she had no idea where it came from because it wasn't in her genetic make-up. Nor was it a strong trait with his father.

"That's not your job," she said, wrapping her arms around the boy who was turning into a young man much too quickly. At 14, Eric was taller than her by at least two inches, but he'd been carrying the burden of her broken heart his entire life. "It's my job to keep him from hurting you," she reminded him.

"Calm your noodles, Mom. I'm not afraid of him," Eric said with all the confidence of a teenage boy who thought he was invincible. "I want to meet him."

It was a conversation they'd had more than once and Jill had promised when Eric made the decision, she'd contact Austin. It wasn't something she'd ever looked forward to.

Jill dug into the bag and pulled out a chip. She smiled when she realized the chip was folded in half. "Wish chip," she said before placing it on her tongue.

"Not fair," Eric groaned, peering into the bag.

Jill closed her eyes, careful not to bite down. It was a silly ritual, but one that she and her son loved. She made her wish, not for herself, but for her son before she smashed the chip with her tongue and enjoyed the salty burst.

"What'd you wish for?" Eric asked.

Jill laughed and ruffled his blond hair. "If I tell you, it won't come true."

Eric responded by filling his mouth with chips and giving another one to Buttercup.

"He's not going to be happy," Jill said, helping herself to

another salty treat. "And it's not about you, you know that. He's going to be angry with me."

"Mom," Eric pleaded. "I can't hide out here forever. Once school starts in a few weeks, people are going to see me and know. I look just like him."

~~~

"You're not dying, are you?" Austin asked after his grandmother threw the ball for her dog.

"Dear God, Austin," she gasped, "what in the world would make you think I'm dying?"

"Nana, you came to France and asked me to grant a dying woman her last wish. That's why I came home."

Nana laughed but Austin didn't see the joke.

"Yes, I did ask you to do that, but I never said I was the dying woman."

If it wasn't Nana, then who … "Sissy?" he asked.

She smiled and Austin knew his grandmother had been scheming with Jill's aunt. "Yes, Sissy. I was just the messenger."

"You left out that little detail," he pointed out, raising an eyebrow even though he knew he held no power over her.

"Would it have mattered?" she asked, obviously knowing it didn't.

"No, I was ready to come home," Austin admitted. Fifteen years traveling the world, working his ass off, and partying it off on the rare occasions when he wasn't working had made him weary. He'd lost the drive to continue adding resorts to his family's dynasty. Austin needed a change, one that included a woman to love and children to take fishing and hiking.

His thoughts drifted to Jill teetering on that ladder, long, tanned legs stretching from under tattered shorts. The frayed strings begged to be tugged, and just thinking about that had somehow thrown her off-balance – or maybe that was her off-key singing. He'd always loved that Jill sang like no one was listening, even when someone was, and the fact she still wore cowgirl boots with any outfit made him smile. When he caught her in his arms, it was like being struck by a lightning bolt. If the shock on Jill's face was any indication, she'd felt the jolt too. For a brief moment he thought she'd forgotten about the past, but then her surprise morphed into anger, or maybe something so much worse.

"Sissy knew what transpired between you and Jill wasn't irreparable. Teens, after all, are quick to jump to conclusions rather than talk through their disagreements." Nana seemed so dismissive of the whole sordid incident. Austin couldn't disagree, at least not from his perspective. After overhearing her mother's demands, Austin didn't even give Jill a chance to explain. He'd simply repeated his father's vile words to Jill and left town, never once looking back.

By the time he had come to his senses, Jill was gone. While he had the means to find her, he didn't think she'd ever forgive him. He also didn't think he deserved her forgiveness, not after the way he treated her. It was easier to let it go than to fight a battle he didn't think he could win.

"Jill hasn't forgiven me," he pointed out, remembering her scowl as she wriggled out of his arms.

Vince placed the ball into Nana's outstretched hand as if he'd been obeying this woman for years and not mere days. "Every relationship has chemistry," she said, tossing the ball once again. The Rottweiler sprinted across the manicured lawn and into the woods where the ball had disappeared. Nana had once played baseball for the All American Girls Baseball league before the franchise disbanded. Even now at 78, she could still throw the ball better than Austin. "Some relationships have good chemistry, some have bad. You and Jill, you were young, but your love was real. That was good chemistry." She turned to Austin and now she was the one raising an eyebrow. "Would you agree?"

Austin nodded as he remembered how perfect Jill felt in his

arms, soft and warm and right.

"But even good chemistry is susceptible to outside influences," Nana continued, turning away to watch for Vince. "Your father and Jill's mother were toxic. When their affair exploded, you and Jill didn't stand a chance. Your chemistry was poisoned because you were too young and innocent to know how to keep the poison out. You needed time and space to let the air clear and grow up."

The air had been clear for Austin for years. He'd long ago realized he was wrong about Jill, that she was a victim of her mother's manipulations and his father's infidelity and judgment. Based on her attitude toward Austin today though, the air hadn't cleared for her.

"She wasn't thrilled to see me," Austin admitted.

Vince returned, but instead of taking the ball from him, Nana poked a long, slender finger into Austin's sternum. "You be persistent and that chemistry you shared will fire up again."

He laughed. "I never knew you were such a romantic." Nana and Grandpa's relationship had always seemed like one of tolerance more than love.

Nana took the ball from Vince and turned to Austin. "Promise me something," she demanded, her smile fading.

His heart dropped into his stomach and Austin fell to his knees. "Anything, Nana. Anything."

And he meant it. She'd always been there for him.

When his father was busy with all of his women and couldn't make time for his son, Nana had taken Austin fishing and to his first baseball game.

When his mother was off shopping for things she didn't need, Nana helped him conjugate verbs and finish his senior project.

When Austin had sputtered hateful words to the girl he loved and sent her running, Nana was there with her strong shoulders and open heart.

Yeah, she was the only one who'd always been there for him and there was nothing he wouldn't do for her.

"Don't settle for just anyone. Fight for the woman you love and don't ever let her go."

Jill, he thought, as a rare tear fell from the corner of his grandmother's eye and slid down her cheek. The only other time Austin had seen his stoic grandmother cry was when they buried his grandfather. Austin was sure then that those had been tears of relief, not sadness.

Now, though, this was sadness.

"Nana, I don't understand," he said, getting to his feet and brushing the lone tear away.

"My marriage was arranged. Your grandfather's family wasn't as wealthy as mine, but your grandfather was smart and ambitious. Those were traits my father was looking for and since he knew I wouldn't pick a smart match, I was forced to marry your grandfather."

"I, I didn't know that," Austin admitted, feeling the same sadness. Nana was such a kind, passionate woman. She deserved more than a forced marriage.

"I was wild. I squandered my father's money for my own fun. I was selfish and irresponsible. Even though I didn't love your grandfather, marrying him was the right decision."

Austin wasn't so sure about that. It sounded more like a punishment than a right decision. His grandfather had been a miserable old coot, but somehow Nana was able to reel in his temper. Well, most of the time.

"And your grandfather was not stupid. He signed a prenup and took my name." She laughed, as if in triumph. "It was unheard of back then for a husband to take his wife's name, but I was the sole heir to my family's dynasty, and my father insisted the name live on. So your grandfather became a Hale in order to be a very rich man."

Rich and controlling, something he'd passed on to his son.

"Your father didn't marry for love either," she said, more somberly. "I won't say bad things to you about Diana, but I'd be lying if I said I liked your mother."

Nodding, Austin bit back any retorts he might have. His mother was a difficult woman to love, never mind like. "I've done the math, Nana. I know she was pregnant before they got married." He'd been born seven months after the wedding and at eight pounds three ounces, he certainly wasn't born premature.

"So this is my charge to you, marry for love."

It wasn't the first time she'd preached those words. He nodded again, wanting that same thing. Austin had only ever been in love once, when he was very young, and under his father's negative influence, he had tossed it away like yesterday's garbage. Austin wasn't the type of man who lived with regret, but hurting Jill Butler was a regret he lived with every day.

"Do you promise?" Nana urged, so serious it scared him.

"Yes, Nana, I promise to marry for love." After what he'd grown up with, Austin wanted nothing less. He just hoped it was in the cards for him.

Her expression softened at his declaration and she wrapped her arms around him in an affectionate embrace. Austin absorbed her love like a dry sponge desperate for water. Nana was the only one in his family who had ever shown him affection.

His mother's hugs were stiff, like a freshly starched shirt that refused to wrinkle. His father's embraces were limited to a rare pat on the shoulder. Even when Austin had completed his first project at age 22, managing the purchase and renovation of a ramshackle resort in Vale, Colorado, Charleston had only said, "Good job." There wasn't a "son" tagged onto that praise, nor an "I'm proud of you." Now, ten resorts later, Austin had given up seeking his father's praise.

"I'm not sure what to do about Jill," he admitted. He'd never had to chase a woman; they flocked to him because of his money and status. While he'd had plenty of lovers, he'd never again loved a woman, not since Jill.

"You're intelligent and charming," Nana smiled, "for which I will take credit. You'll find a way to earn her forgiveness and win her love."

Chapter 2

WHEN JILL SNEEZED FOR THE fortieth time in the last half hour, she decided enough was enough. "We have to do something about all these cats," she insisted.

"How many did you wrangle up?" Cathlynn Merriweather, AKA, Cat, AKA Jill's childhood best friend, asked as one of the furry felines wove between Cat's ankles.

"Twenty-seven and counting," Jill sighed, tossing her notebook on the reception desk.

In an attempt to get a grasp on the animal and financial situation of the rescue, Jill had been milling through the paper files for hours, but most of the cats weren't documented.

"Oh, God, I hope they are all spayed and neutered," Jill prayed.

Cat laughed. "Sissy didn't believe in freedom of reproduction, remember?"

Jill relaxed and laughed along. Sissy thought the world was overpopulated and had crazy ideas about couples having to apply for a license in order to reproduce. She felt the same way about the animals she rescued.

Sadness rushed through Jill. How could Sissy be gone? Jill promised to visit, but the promises went unfulfilled as she found any reason to avoid the memories this town would stir when she came back. Sissy never pressured her, but Jill would give anything to see her aunt one more time.

"People visited her when she was sick. How could no one have known she had that many cats in the house?" Cat asked.

Jill shrugged and tried to ignore the guilt that once again reared its ugly head. If only Sissy had told Jill she was dying, Jill would have come home and taken care of her, and the cat situation.

"The Barn is overcrowded," Jill sighed. "All the kennels are full. Some are doubled and tripled up. There's no way I can house another cat in here." She batted her eyelashes, whining like a puppy dog.

"Oh no," Cat moaned, her head shaking like a bobble head on a bumpy road. "No more cats for me." The fuzz ball rubbed up against Cat's leg as if pleading to be taken home.

"Come on, Cat. This is ridiculous. What am I supposed to do with all these cats?"

A sinister smile crossed her friend's lips. "You could keep a few."

Eric had suggested the same thing. That kid would keep all the animals if she'd let him. Jill stroked the dog sitting obediently next to her. "You planning to buy stock in allergy meds?" she quipped.

"Those things last for twenty-four hours. One a day isn't a big deal."

"I almost died just cleaning Sissy's house." After all, it was the sneeze that caused her to fall off the ladder, and that was after she'd taken her meds. Jill didn't want to spend her life fighting off allergic reactions to the animals she wished she could love a little more closely.

Cat glanced at her watch. "It's early. We can do an adoption and foster drive today, put out a Facebook blast on the town's page about needing foster homes. That will help get the shelter situation under control."

Jill spun around in the office chair. "Oh, Cat, I don't know …"

Asking the townspeople for help? Jill wasn't ready for that. She'd only been in town a week and had kept a very low profile. It was best to reintroduce herself slowly and hope her name didn't trigger any scandalous memories.

"No one cares, Jilly," Cat rolled her eyes. "I doubt anyone even remembers what happened. Old man Hale has been dead for a decade and his asshole son hasn't been back since the funeral."

"You remember," Jill reminded her.

"Only because you were my best friend and you disappeared. I went in search of information."

"Information that you got from the rumor mill in town." Jill doubted that rumor mill had changed, or forgotten.

"So what? The mighty Charleston Hale called you a promiscuous little slut," Cat whined in a dramatic voice that made Jill feel stupid for letting it bother her. "Everyone knew it wasn't true."

The problem was, Charleston hadn't been the only one to call her that. Jill wondered how many people knew Austin had repeated his father's words.

"Claudia is still here," Jill added. There was no way the matriarch of the Hale dynasty didn't have all the details. Once she found out about Eric, she might be angry enough to drive the band-wagon that smeared Jill's name all over town.

"Well, lucky for you, Claudia loves animals. She was Sissy's most generous patron."

Maybe so, but she wasn't the only Hale to worry about. "Austin is back, too."

"With his smoldering stare and heroic arms," Cat cooed, making Jill regret she'd told Cat about Austin showing up at the house.

But Austin hadn't said anything about the past. In fact, until she'd given him the cold shoulder, he'd been nice.

"They may be nice now, but they won't be once they find out

about Eric," Jill said.

"Yeah, well, you dug that grave."

When Jill reconnected with Cat several years back, her best friend had been both happy and angry that Jill had dropped off the face of the earth for so long. While she'd promised to keep Jill's secret, she made it known time and again she didn't approve.

There was no avoiding this. Jill had made the conscious decision to return to Lilac Ridge. She had to hold on to the faith that the town had forgotten the scandal she'd been at the heart of.

"Do you really think we can find foster homes for all of them?" Jill asked as Cat pounded away on the laptop.

"Think positive, sister. If nothing else, we can play the sympathy card. Sissy was eccentric, but everyone in this town loved her. They also loved you. They'll come to your rescue."

Jill didn't want to be rescued. She'd learned to stand on her own two feet and not rely on anyone. For the last fourteen years she'd raised her son without help. She was someone who got things done. Being back in Lilac Ridge seemed to be stripping that confidence from her.

Cat pulled out her phone. "Who are you calling?" Jill asked.

"Courtney Daniels. She volunteers here and will be able to lend a hand."

Twenty minutes later, while Jill printed blank applications and foster home agreements, Courtney skipped into the office at the front of the Barn. "I'm so excited you're doing this. Those animals need homes. They've been in those kennels far too long."

"What are you talking about?" Jill asked.

Courtney hesitated, then stuck out her hand. "Courtney Daniels."

Jill shook the young woman's hand. "Jill Butler, Sissy's niece."

"I'm sorry about Sissy. She was really great."

"Thanks," Jill said, but something went unsaid and Jill needed to get to the bottom of it. "What do you mean the animals have been in the Barn too long?"

Courtney sighed. "Sorry, but Sissy, well, there's no easy way to say this. She got a little crazy near the end. I don't know if it was the tumor or dementia or what, but she got real picky about homing the animals. She turned more people away than she allowed to adopt. I tried to talk to her about it, but if she didn't brush me off, she'd yell at me. I didn't want to fight with her and even though I'm just a volunteer, I didn't want to lose my position, so I let it go."

"Well, we're going to set it right," Jill insisted, brushing aside the guilt about not being there for Sissy. Of course, since her aunt didn't bother to inform anyone until it was too late, there wasn't a whole lot Jill could have done.

But this, this is what she did. Since earning her degree six years ago, she'd been working as a project manager for a small software company. There wasn't a problem she couldn't fix. She just had to approach this whole rescue situation as a new project. "These are all the files I could find on the animals. Not all of them are accounted for."

Courtney smiled and reached into her messenger bag, pulling out a tablet. "Sissy was old school, preferred everything on paper, but I convinced her to go paperless. Sold her on the whole environmental angle. I've got everyone right here."

Jill was impressed. "You're just a volunteer?"

"I'm in college. I get credit for working here, but I'd do it anyway. I love the animals."

There were a lot of animals. As Courtney opened a database, Jill saw the list of animals by type: dogs, cats, ferrets … oh, dear God. "Snakes? Sissy took in snakes?"

Courtney smiled. "They're difficult to home. She's had these two for months. I don't know how she could afford to keep them. If the rescue isn't homing animals, it isn't bringing in any homing fees."

"Courtney, where are the snakes?" Jill asked with a shaky voice. She had been in the Barn every day for the past week to care for the animals. There were no snakes.

"She has them in glass cages in her cellar. It's more temperate there than in the Barn."

Jill had been cleaning that house for a week, and had started sleeping there two days ago, but she hadn't worked up the courage to go into the cellar. As a child, she'd been terrified to go down there. The dirt floor made it smell musty and appealed to creepy critters. After a face off with a giant frog when she was ten, Jill refused to step foot down there.

"They were last fed a few days after Sissy died," Courtney said, "so they are definitely due for a feeding."

Shaking off the shiver threatening to race up her spine, Jill offered Courtney a warm smile. "You can take care of that, right?"

Courtney barked out a sardonic laugh. "I'm a volunteer, but even if I got paid, you couldn't pay me to do that. I had to bribe my brother to feed them. He's a six foot tall, 230 pound wall of muscle who rides a Harley, has tattoos and carves wood with a chainsaw, but it freaked him out. He's been screaming like a girl in his sleep every night."

Jill laughed. "You're making that up."

"So not," Courtney insisted. "There's a freezer in the cellar where Sissy keeps a supply of food."

The bell attached to the door rang and they all looked up to find a father and child walking in, both looking eager.

"Hi," Courtney greeted them. "How can we help you?"

~~~

Jill was ready to collapse.

It seemed everyone in town had stopped by, and even people from neighboring Sunset Valley thanks to Cat sending a message to the veterinarian there, who had blasted the fostering event from their Facebook page and their e-mail list.

"I smell like cat," Cat complained, falling onto the small bench in the waiting area of the office.

More than half of the cats had been adopted and many more fostered. Three dogs had also been adopted, six more fostered, and someone had taken one of the snakes, cage and all. Jill had waived the homing fee on that one and hid in the back of the Barn while Eric took the guy to the cellar and helped him get the snake out through the bulkhead at the back of the house.

"Oh, good," Courtney said, looking out the office window. "Our biggest supporter is here."

Jill couldn't imagine there was a bigger supporter than the people who had passed through already, but she was happy nonetheless. Exhaustion was irrelevant. The more animals she could find good forever homes for, the better.

She gasped when the patron walked in the door.

"Claudia," Courtney cooed. "Thanks so much for coming."

"It's my pleasure, dear. Vince is a bit lonely. I should have been back sooner to find him a friend, but, well, it fell by the wayside during Sissy's final days."

Claudia Hale was a beautiful, elegant woman. Her casual look, which put Jill's professional look to shame, was comprised of loose-fitting linen pants and a matching cap-sleeved linen blouse. She wore a large-brimmed hat with real flowers on the brim. "Jillian, dear, so good to see you again. I'm sorry for your loss. Sissy was a lovely woman."

"Thank you, Mrs. Hale," Jill bit out, trying to swallow her anxiety over seeing the Hale matriarch. It was a good thing Eric was staked out in the cellar, completely enthralled with the remaining snake he'd dubbed Mr. Slither. Just the name sent a chill racing up Jill's spine, as did the thought of Claudia seeing the great-grandson she didn't even know about.

Jill knew he couldn't hide out in the cellar forever, but she wanted to tell Austin about Eric before anyone else saw him. Eric was right, he did look just like Austin. It wouldn't take a genius to do the math on his age and figure out who his father was.

"Oh, goodness, you're not a child anymore. Call me Claudia.

Mrs. Hale makes me feel so old and I'd like to think I have many prosperous years left."

All Jill could do was nod because she wasn't sure she'd ever be able to call the woman by her first name, at least not to her face. Claudia had always been kind to Jill, even when her husband and son had tried to keep her from seeing Austin. Jill never knew if the kindness was genuine or if it was a facade to keep up appearances, but her gut told her Claudia Hale was an ally.

Fortunately Courtney stepped in. "Let me show you the dogs. We have one that I think you'll just love."

Not realizing she'd been holding her breath, Jill let it out after Courtney and Claudia disappeared into the part of the barn that housed the dogs.

"See," Cat said. "I told you no one cares."

"I'm not sure my heart is ever going to slow down," she admitted. She didn't want to look a gift horse in the mouth, but it did seem to go well. She just hoped when Claudia and Austin learned about Eric it would be just as friendly. "She was always very nice to me."

"It's because you're a good person. You can't be blamed for what your mother did."

Of course she could because most people didn't know what really happened. They only had Charleston and Austin's version of the story, and neither of their perspectives put Jill or her family in a good light.

"It's almost five. As soon as we close the doors, you want to grab dinner? I want to run some ideas by you."

"Of course. Ideas for what?" Cat asked.

"Fund-raisers for this place. I've looked at the books and I don't know how Sissy kept this place going. Adoption fees aren't going to keep it running. I need to generate funds to keep it afloat."

"Claudia wants to adopt Einstein," Courtney said, startling Jill. She spun in the chair to see the two women standing on the other side of the desk, Claudia holding a leash. Jill leaned forward to find a boxer on the other end.

Jill had gotten comfortable with the database during their marathon adoption and foster fest, so she pulled up Einstein's file on the computer and checked the customer database to see if Claudia was already in it. "You've adopted from Sissy before," Jill said when she found Claudia's record.

Claudia simply nodded. The history was long and now that Jill thought about it, she remembered always seeing Claudia with a dog. The records showed she always adopted older, large breed dogs, just like Einstein.

"You look surprised, dear," Claudia said.

"No, I'm just, well, these dogs probably wouldn't have been adopted. You saved them."

"I'm an old lady. I've never had patience for puppies. These older dogs require a lot of love and I have the means to provide that, so I'm happy to."

Cat and Courtney focused their attention on Einstein while Jill worked with Claudia to complete the proverbial paperwork. She'd managed to create an online form that could be filled out on the computer and digitally signed. It was going to save loads in paper and printer ink. "We ask for a donation of $100 to help cover the expenses."

"I know the drill, dear. I told Sissy $100 isn't enough. You need to consider raising your fees and making them a requirement, not a donation."

Claudia pushed a check across the counter and Jill had to swallow her gasp. "Mrs. Hale, this is—"

"Very generous of me, very kind, yes, yes. The fact is, I come from a family who has always squandered our excessive wealth. I've made an effort since my grandson was born to not take for granted what we have and frankly, dear, what Sissy built here is a worthy cause."

Jill wanted to say no to the check, that it was too much, but the Barn needed the money and as Claudia had pointed out, the Hales had it in excessive amounts.

"Thank you," Jill said, tucking the $3000 check into the money bag. She'd added a cash register to the list of things to purchase. Maybe this check could go toward that.

"Oh, and when you decide on a fund-raiser, the Hale will be happy to host the event at no charge," Claudia continued. "Might I suggest a singles auction? The alumni association held one last year and it was quite successful." Claudia pulled a business card out of her purse. "This is the direct number to The Hale's events manager. Tell her I told you to call."

"Thank you," Jill managed to say again without stammering.

"You're very welcome. I assume I'll be seeing you at the house this week?"

When Jill looked at Claudia like she had three heads, the woman laughed. "To do the home visit before you approve my grandson to adopt a dog?"

Austin.

Jill had tried to forget about his application. She didn't want to deal with Austin. Seeing him just once had thrown Jill completely off-balance — sneezing on a rickety ladder not withstanding — and she hadn't quite regained her equilibrium.

"Right, a home check. I'm not sure it'll be me doing that," Jill explained, hoping she could get Courtney to take on that task.

"Well, Austin has moved into the gate house, thank goodness. The last thing an old woman needs is her young grandson slogging around her house. Do come up to the main house and say hello. You can check on Vince and Einstein while you're there."

"Of course," Jill said, her head spinning. Before she could take a breath, Claudia commanded Einstein to "come" and swept out of the Barn as if she hadn't just paid $3000 for an old dog and offered her upscale resort for a fund-raiser.

Chapter 3

AUSTIN STOMPED INTO THE BARN like a little kid who hadn't gotten his way, because of course, he hadn't gotten his way. Jill was ignoring him and that pissed him off.

"Where's Jillian?" he demanded when the door slammed behind him.

A young woman with curly brown hair peered at him over a laptop. "She's cleaning kennels. I can call her—"

"I know my way around," he dismissed her and headed toward the door that led to the kennels. Austin had grown up here. When he was just 13, Nana insisted he find a worthy cause and start volunteering his time and his skills. Austin wasn't sure he had any skills at the time, but he loved dogs and given he was growing up in a town that was entirely too small for the only heir to a vast legacy, the Barn seemed like the best place to hide out. Because Lilac Ridge was such a small town, he recognized Jillian Butler immediately, but hadn't realized her connection to the animal rescue. He soon learned Sissy was Jill's mother's aunt.

He'd spent the next six years volunteering at the Barn. Jill became an ally because even though her parents weren't wealthy like his, they spent their lives ignoring their only daughter. It didn't take long before Jill was his best friend, and then his first love.

His only love.

As Austin entered the kennel area, dogs stirred, a few barking, some whining as he made his way past them. Though he wanted to confront Jill now, he slowed and calmed his steps, checking out the dogs who needed homes. There wasn't an empty kennel. Too many dogs needed homes. Since Austin was willing, the situation here just confirmed that Jill was making him jump through hoops simply because she could.

He heard water running and headed in the direction of the grooming station in the northeast corner. He found Jill, drenched and covered in muck, washing a golden retriever.

Worn denim hugged her soft curves. A form-fitting white t-shirt covered the top of her body. Her long dark hair was pulled into a pony tail. She'd worn it all one length when they were kids, but now she had a thick spray of bangs that played up the innocence of her pretty face.

"You're a naughty girl," Jill said with little conviction as she massaged soap all through the dog's coat.

As if in protest to Jill's proclamation, the dog shook, spraying water and suds in every direction like a sprinkler hooked to a hose. Austin was just out of range, but Jill was at ground zero and ended up even more drenched.

Austin couldn't help but laugh and when he did, Jill turned in a rage. Somehow her anger seemed to calm his. "Need some help?" he asked as he came up next to her.

"You're not supposed to be back here without an escort," she snarled. Austin couldn't be sure if she was pissed he was back there or because she'd just been the victim of a wet dog sprinkler.

"I'm back here with you," he pointed out.

Austin couldn't resist, he gave her the once over. The white shirt was completely see-through, revealing sexy lingerie beneath the

26

cotton covering. "I've always been a fan of zebra print," he drawled, focusing on the round swells beneath the wet shirt.

She tugged the shirt from her body, but the image of her round, zebra covered breasts was already imprinted in his mind.

"What do you want, Austin?" she huffed.

"Let me help," he insisted, prying the spray hose from her fingers. "If I recall correctly, this kind of job works better with two people."

They'd done this before. Part of their job as teen volunteers was to wash the animals. Jill must have remembered because she didn't fight him. Instead, she held the dog firmly at her shoulders and spoke sweet, soft reassurances while Austin rinsed all the suds off. When his hand brushed Jill's, first by complete circumstance, then deliberately, the subtle contact sent a surge of awareness through him.

He wanted more. Not just the physical contact, but the emotional connection they'd shared when they were friends, and when their relationship had grown to so much more.

When the suds were gone, Austin pointed the spray at Jill, giving her a good hose down and further revealing the zebra print bra. He wondered if the panties matched.

Jill squealed and hopped back. "Austin! What the hell!"

Austin smirked. "You looked like you needed a bath, too."

She pinned him with a stern expression he knew she was struggling to maintain. It had always been this way with them. They survived all their trials and tribulations through laughter and friendship and their mutual love of the animals in this shelter.

And later, through their mutual love of each other.

"I have a dozen kennels to clean and countless dogs to wash," she drawled. "I'll get my bath later."

Hmmm … would she entertain company for that?

"Alone," she scowled, reading his wayward thoughts.

"I can help," he said, not wanting to leave. While today may not be the best time to talk about anything significant, Austin had felt he'd cracked the ice wall around Jill and he didn't want to give it a chance to ice back over.

Jill's expression softened as she seemed to contemplate his offer, but it wasn't long before the scowl returned. "You didn't come here to wash dogs. What do you want?"

He wanted Jill to forgive him, and let him take her to dinner, but Austin wasn't naive. He knew that wasn't in the cards today.

"I came to check on my application status. I thought you'd call by now to set up the home visit."

A range of emotions passed across her face, but they were gone before Austin could pinpoint any of them. "It's been busy here. I'm still trying to get familiar with all of our procedures."

"My grandmother adopted a dog the other day," he pointed out. He had been shocked when he'd strolled up to the manor to find another dog chasing a ball in the back yard.

"Your grandmother has already been approved to adopt," she said.

"Are you being a hard ass about this because of what hap–"

"It's procedure," she interjected. "I can't make exceptions for you just because you're rich. Some people might bend over backwards because you're a Hale, but I'm not one of those people."

She'd never been one of those people. Nor had she been one to bully him because she assumed he was a spoiled rich kid. Had it been up to Austin's father, he would have been shipped off to boarding school when he was eight, but it was Nana who insisted Austin stay in Lilac Ridge and grow up as a normal kid. At the time it had sucked because of the bullies, but in hindsight, it made Austin appreciate all he'd had to work for.

"I wouldn't expect you to be," he said, closing the space between them.

"Back off. You'll get wet."

He wanted to get wet, to melt the ice around her and find the girl he'd loved inside. She backed against the wall and Austin followed, pinning her between his arms. Her eyes widened and as his gaze shifted to her soft lips, her tongue darted out.

Austin accepted the silent invitation. Lowering his head, he closed his eyes, bracing himself for the onslaught of emotions sure to accompany the kiss. Instead of finding her lips, he met a cold and aggressive spray of water.

Jumping back, he tried to escape the spray, but Jill was relentless. It was only when he cut the water off at the source that the unexpected shower stopped.

Jill smiled, a sardonic grin that showed her satisfaction at getting Austin back. "I warned you," she chuckled.

He was soaked to the bone, his jeans weighing him down, but he didn't care. It may have been payback, but he also took it as a positive sign.

"Now that I'm as drenched as you, I may as well stay and help around here. Where do you want me to start?" he asked.

Jill rolled her eyes. "You'll need to sign a volunteer waiver."

"Jilly,"

"It's Jill," she corrected again, the amusement gone from her eyes. The ice queen had returned. Good thing Austin wasn't a quitter.

"Fine, I'll jump through your hoops. Where's the waiver."

"It's not hoops, Austin. This is my rescue now. If you don't sign a waiver, I'm liable if something happens. I don't have endless financial capacity like you do to deal with something like that."

There she was, throwing his family's wealth in his face again. She'd never been like that. Since he'd acted like the spoiled rich kid while her family fell apart, he figured he deserved it.

"If it means protecting you, I'm happy to sign anything."

She rolled her eyes and directed him back to the reception desk. "You can start in the cellar," she said.

"Still afraid to go down there?"

Her smile returned, making Austin's heart skip a few beats. "The bulkhead is unlocked. You'll find whatever you need for cleaning supplies—"

"In the storage room just off the reception area. I know the drill." He'd done this before. Since the Barn looked the same, except maybe a little weathered with time, he didn't figure any of the procedures had changed.

"I'll leave you to it then," she said and walked away.

Austin returned to the reception desk and signed the waiver. He didn't know what to expect in the cellar, so he decided to inspect the space before grabbing any supplies.

The bulkhead might have been unlocked, but it was old and rusty and a bitch to tug open. He left the door open for ventilation because he remembered it was always musty, and descended the stairs.

The crumbling foundation was built of stone, not unlike the old farmhouses scattered around Lilac Ridge. Austin had seen enough decrepit buildings over the last fifteen years to know this one needed to be replaced. He was working with a contractor on the new headquarters for Hale Enterprises, maybe he could get Jill a good price on the work. He'd pay for it outright, but Austin doubted she would let him.

He stepped across the dirt floor, wondering if Jill would be willing to come down here with a new foundation that included a concrete floor. As his eyes scanned the room, he stopped short, his heart plunging into his stomach. "Son of a bitch," he muttered.

Very few things scared Austin. In fact, only one living thing did and it didn't matter that a glass cage kept it confined.

That's why Jill had smiled when she said he could clean the cellar.

Pulling in some deep breaths through his nose, he tried not to be pissed off. He'd hurt Jill and deserved a little payback, but tricking him into the cellar with a caged snake was downright cruel.

After storming out of the cellar and across the yard, he ignored the woman at the reception desk and sought out Jill. She was cleaning a kennel, the golden retriever napping at her feet.

"That was mean," Austin growled.

Jill smiled, clearly amused. "You said you wanted to help."

"You know how much I hate snakes."

She scratched the dog's ear, holding Austin's stare as her smile faded. "It didn't keep you from turning into one."

She obviously wanted a fight, and so did Austin. He'd come here ready for one, only to be assuaged when seeing her washing the dog.

"Is this Buttercup?" he asked, wondering if this was the dog his grandmother had mentioned, the one Jill said was already adopted.

"Yes." It was another curt response, making Austin wonder how long it was going to take to break through the ice wall she'd erected around herself.

"I thought she'd been adopted."

The comment earned Austin another of Jill's sneers. "I adopted her."

Jill's spite surged through him as if he'd been struck by lightning. "Was that before or after I inquired about her?" he asked. Well, he'd tried to ask, but it came out more as a demand. He was still wound up about his face to face with that snake. Plus, if she was going to be difficult, he was going to call her out on it. The Jill he knew wasn't manipulative, but her mother was. He hoped she hadn't gone down that path.

"This is my shelter now. I'm responsible for these animals. I won't have you charging in and accusing me of anything."

"I'm not ..." but he stopped because she was right. Jill obviously still had an ax to grind with him, which was fair given how he'd hurt her. Austin had hoped enough time had passed that Jill had put it behind her.

He boxed her in again, this time checking her hands to make sure she wasn't armed with the hose. "Austin," she whispered as her eyes closed and that one word was music to his ears. He pressed his mouth to hers, sweeping his tongue across her lips. It was a question she answered by parting her lips and gripping the front of his shirt.

It was like being sucked into a tornado and before Austin could stop himself, he was pressed against her, thigh to chest, his arms wrapped around her back and holding her steady.

Maybe he was holding himself steady.

Jill was right there with him, her soft moans vibrating against his lips, her hands clinging to his shoulders.

As quickly as the storm had started, Jill turned away. "Stop," she whispered. Even though it was a quiet plea, not one filled with indignation, Austin stepped back, putting a little air between them.

"I'm not here to hurt you," he promised, the words he'd meant to say before losing control. Taking another step back, he hoped Jill would hear the sincerity in his voice.

"You don't have the power to hurt me," she said with an air of confidence that was a direct stab to Austin's heart.

He didn't want to hurt her, not ever again, but if he didn't have the power to hurt her, it meant she'd never open her heart to him. He thought of his grandmother's encouraging words, to use his intelligence and charm to win Jill's forgiveness. Forgiveness wasn't enough. He wanted to win her love.

Because after all the time and space, as Nana had put it, Austin knew he still loved this woman who had been the only one to ever own his heart.

Closing the distance between them in two long, sure steps, Austin cupped her face in his hands, forcing her to meet his eyes. "You have the power to hurt me, Jilly. I just hope you'll give me a chance to prove I am not my father's son."

~~~

Days later, that kiss remained at the forefront of Jill's thoughts. As she washed the breakfast dishes, scrubbing non-existent food remnants as if a clean plate would give her a clean slate and wash away the memory of the kiss that still made her all gooey inside, she watched Eric at the computer. Occasionally he would glance her way and Jill would smile, but Eric didn't smile back. He was focused on whatever it was on the screen. Jill worried he was cyber-stalking his father again.

"Stop stalking me," Eric mumbled.

"I'm not stalking, I'm staring. There's a difference," Jill defended.

"You're weirding me out," Eric confessed.

Jill laughed. "What are you looking at?" she dared ask.

Eric glanced at her and back at the screen before a sinister smile that was all Hale stretched his mouth. "Snakes."

A shiver raced up and back down her spine with Eric's words, then once again as she remembered what lived in the cellar.

Eric's fascination with snakes was not Hale. It wasn't Butler either. Since Sissy was the one who took the snakes in, the snake affection must come from the Barnes side of the family, and had skipped a couple generations.

"Sorry I asked," Jill murmured, turning off the water and grabbing a towel to dry the dishes.

"Mr. Slither is a king snake. Once he gets used to me, I might be able to hold him and he'll wrap himself right around my arm." Eric's excitement was lost on Jill.

"I haven't agreed to let you keep him," Jill reminded her son.

"I'll keep him in the cellar. I promise. You won't even know he's there."

No, not until he escaped and slithered up the stairs where he'd wrap himself around Jill's neck and suffocate her in her sleep.

"We kept Buttercup, bud. We can't keep every animal that comes through here. It defeats the purpose of the Barn."

The apple didn't fall far from the tree. When Jill was a kid, she wanted to adopt every animal her aunt rescued. Jill's parents, however, were not accommodating. They didn't let her adopt a single animal from the rescue.

When he looked at her with those sky-blue eyes, though, Jill wasn't able to tell him no. He'd sacrificed too much, more than a kid should have to. Instead of fight with him, or give in to his pleading eyes, Jill changed the subject.

"What are your plans for the day?"

Eric clicked the mouse a few times before heading to the fridge. He poured a glass of milk and joined Jill at the long bar where she settled in with her second cup of coffee. "I was hoping you'd take me to meet him today."

Jill didn't miss how Eric still referred to Austin in third person. She understood why he hadn't embraced Austin as Dad or even his father yet, given the fact he was 14 and had never even met the man. Eric also wouldn't refer to his father by first name. Jill suspected it was his way of keeping some distance even though it was obvious he didn't want to.

She took a long sip of coffee, hoping a valid reason not to introduce Eric and Austin would pop into her head, but Eric's pleading eyes crushed and brilliant ideas before they formed. Instead, she went with the honest, though somewhat lame, excuse. "I need to tell him first, bud."

"It's been a week since he showed up here."

"I know, but it's not that easy."

Eric's eyes narrowed and darkened with fury. "He can't hurt you. Whatever he says, whatever he does, he can't. I won't let him, Mom, not ever again."

If only it were that sample. Jill wasn't worried about Austin hurting her. There was nothing he could say or do to her that could be worse than what he'd done 15 years ago. He could hurt Eric, though, and that wasn't something she was about to let happen.

"Come here," she said, turning on her bar stool.

"Mom," he whined.

"Come here," she said again. This time Eric slid out of his chair and into her arms.

He'd grown so much, no longer the little boy she worked so hard to protect and teach right from wrong. Her life had changed the night she left Lilac Ridge, but little did she know it had changed before that. She'd been terrified when she found out she was pregnant, but Eric was the best part of her life.

"Just give me some time, okay? I promise, I'll tell him when the time is right." The problem was, Jill knew the time would never be right.

Chapter 4

FOR OVER TWO WEEKS JILL managed to avoid going into town. Sissy's property was three miles out of Lilac Ridge on the way to Sunset Valley, a town that could provide for all her needs much more safely than Lilac Ridge.

Now, though, she had a meeting with Melody Starr, the Hale's events manager, to finalize the details for the fund-raiser. Melody insisted they meet in her office at the Hale and Jill couldn't come up with a reasonable excuse not to.

So she put on her big girl panties and headed into town.

No big deal. Everyone had to face their demons at some point. Maybe if Jill did this, drove by the property where she'd grown up, and stepped onto the grounds owned by the family who had torn hers apart, she could finally put it all behind her.

Because the ghosts still followed her, no matter how far she ventured away from this place.

Austin's words from a few days ago haunted her, too.

You have the power to hurt me, Jilly. I just hope you'll give me a chance to prove I am not my father's son.

He had never been his father's son, at least not until that night when her world had come crashing down.

Jill cranked up the music and shook of the doom and gloom. It was all in the past and her motto was to keep moving forward.

Despite the abandoned railroad tracks being converted into a walking and ATV trail, approaching them wasn't any less daunting.

The old tracks separated the town. It was unspoken, but everyone knew if you lived on the south side of the tracks, you were from the wrong side. That's where Jill had spent the first 18 years of her life, in a modest home that was always in disrepair because her father spent all his time doing repairs at the resort and her mother apparently spent all her time running around with Charleston Hale.

Even now, living at Sissy's house, Jill was still from the wrong side of the tracks. The old stigma burrowed its way into her gut and set up residence, amplified by her destination.

At least she didn't have to see her old house. It had gone up in smoke that night, burning to the ground and turning everything in it to cinder and ash. Including her parents.

Jill approached the old railroad crossing slowly. The rails were gone — the old tracks now serving as an ATV trail — but the road was still elevated and she lifted her feet off the floor out of habit, her toes still pressing lightly on the accelerator. She resisted the urge to look down Railroad Street where her old house had been. She would need to go there eventually, just for some closure, but at the moment her biggest task was crossing the tracks.

After reaching the north side, Jill set her heels down and breathed a sigh of relief. She wasn't sure what other outcome there was to worry about. It's not like she'd go up in a poof of smoke or disintegrate into ash just for crossing into the north side of Lilac Ridge.

On this side of the tracks, the town came alive. Main Street ran adjacent to the tracks. The brick buildings were filled with eclectic shops and restaurants that thrived because of the rich patrons of the Hale. That's why the Hale family was put on such a high pedestal.

If the resort ever shut down, the town would die.

Fortunately for Lilac Ridge, Claudia Hale was kind and generous. Her husband, however, had been a vengeful old man who thought every person in this town should bow to his every demand. Their son hadn't been any different, though rather than squandering his money on fancy cars, he spent it on his mistresses.

Jill maneuvered her Ford Focus east on Main Street toward the Hale. The resort sat perched halfway up Hale Mountain and overlooked the town. It had been a popular family resort until the 1960's when that type of family vacation became less popular. That was when it had undergone extensive renovations to cater to the wealthy. With its 18-hole golf course and direct access to skiing in the winter and an alpine slide and zip line in the summer, as well as a gondola that carried riders to the lookout at the top of the mountain, it was a year round-resort.

The road leading off Main Street was long and winding. If Jill wasn't dreading stepping onto the Hale property, knowing it was going to be a hailstorm of memories, she might enjoy the scenic vista. Her nerves were too shaky for any enjoyment. The last time she'd been on this property, she'd gotten her father fired and set off a series of events that spiraled out of control so fast she still felt like she'd survived a tornado.

As she pulled into what was now the business lot at the southwest corner of the Hale, the tornado tugged her in once again.

She smiled at the challenge she had issued Austin, that they christen every guest room in the Hale. Not only was it exciting to be with Austin, but sneaking around in the grand hotel, knowing their fathers could be anywhere and they could get caught made it even more exciting.

When Charleston caught them having sex in one of the guest rooms, he dragged them into old man Hale's office on the fourth floor. To Jill's horror, they'd summoned her father who was the maintenance foreman at the resort. After a lot of yelling between all three Hale men, Austin had been forbidden to see Jill, which was ridiculous since he was 19 and living at the gate house when he wasn't off at college. When Austin simply smirked at his father and grandfather and challenged them to keep him away from Jill, they'd turned the tables and fired her father.

Her father made her wait in the car — parked in almost the same spot where Jill now sat and stared at the windows of that fourth floor office — while he stayed and tried to convince old man Hale to let him keep his job. Apparently his pleas didn't work, or fell on deaf ears as Austin had said, because when her father finally joined her in the car, he dumped all of his tools in the trunk.

He'd given Jill the silent treatment. What could he say? Jill was eighteen, about to head to college. She and Austin weren't doing anything illegal and while it might have been reckless, they were in love.

Hope echoed in the car when they spotted Charleston's car parked in front of the house. Unfortunately, that hope was stomped out when they walked in to find Charleston and her mother having sex. It had seemed violent, her mother bent over the couch, Charleston swearing as he pounded into her, tugging her hair. Jill had screamed, thinking her mother was being raped by the man who had just fired her father. Then her mother yelled at Jill, told her to get out, that she ruined everything.

Her mother had gone ghost white when Jill's father walked in.

And if Jill thought the sex seemed violent, it was nothing compared to what her father unleashed on Charleston.

Sitting in her car now, fifteen years later, Jill couldn't shake the terror she'd felt that night. Unable to bear the violence, Jill had rushed into the woods and found the path to the Barn. Once there, she climbed the ladder to the loft all the way up in the eaves, hoping to find Austin there, but the loft was empty.

"It's the past. It's done. Keep moving forward," she preached, pulling herself from the storm before it raged out of control. This wasn't the time for a walk down Horror Lane. She had a business meeting. The Hale was just an old building. Sure, it was home to countless ghosts, but Jill didn't need to have dinner with them.

The resort looked newer than she remembered and she realized it wasn't just a fresh coat of paint but a completely different color. The resort had always been white, but now it was a bright yellow, like sunshine.

She pushed whatever remained of the doom and gloom aside with a smile and a deep breath and made her way to the side entrance where the business offices were housed.

"You must be Jill," a smiling woman about Jill's same age greeted her. "I'm Melody. Welcome to the Hale."

Jill simply thanked her, not interested in revealing she'd practically grown up at the resort.

The office was luxurious and spacious, nestled in the corner of the building and overlooking the golf course with a view of the White Mountains. Jill had never been in this particular office. Her fate, and her father's fate had been dealt three floors above.

Jill shook off the shiver and took the seat Melody offered on a sofa in the middle of the room. Melody joined her and flipped open a folder sitting on the glass table in front of the leather sofa.

"I scheduled the event for next Friday," Melody said cheerfully.

"What? How is that possible?" Jill said. It was Tuesday now. Next Friday seemed so close.

"This is what I do. We already have radio spots and I've got two actors and three musicians who have agreed to the auction. I've also recruited some of Lilac Ridge's most eligible bachelors and bachelorettes. Austin refused, unfortunately."

Had he refused because of that kiss?

That kiss.

It had rocked Jill to the core, once again throwing her off-balance. She hadn't intended to let it happen, but she didn't have the hose during his second attempt and it had been impossible to find the words to tell him to stop or the power to move away.

"I'm hoping he'll bid on someone," Melody continued, completely unaware Jill was lost in that memory from a few days ago. "I've also entered myself in the auction."

While Jill was relieved Austin wasn't up for bid, she didn't like the implication of Melody's declaration. Was the woman hoping her boss would bid on her?

Was Melody the reason Austin had moved back to Lilac Ridge?

No, she couldn't be. Austin wouldn't have kissed Jill if Melody was in the picture. Unless he'd become just like his philandering father.

Swallowing the rising anxiety, Jill focused on the task at hand. "What do you need from me?" she asked.

"Nothing, really. Since I've planned one of these before, it was easy. Claudia suggested the name, so we're going with Don't Date the Dog."

Nearly choking on her own laughter, Jill worked hard to pull herself together. "You're kidding, right?" It was a terrible name.

"Not kidding. It's clever and ties in to the shelter. Claudia just loves dogs." Melody spoke of the matriarch like they were best friends. Or maybe Melody was hoping to land the woman as a grandmother-in-law.

Not liking her catty attitude, Jill took a deep breath and smiled. "What about food?" Jill asked.

Melody spent the next thirty minutes going over the menu, the cash bar selections, and the auction items being donated by local businesses.

"That's, just, wow. I don't know what to say. This is amazing. Thank you so much." Jill hadn't expected this. With the scandal fifteen years ago that had her family destroying the peaceful climate of this small town, Jill didn't expect to be welcomed back with open arms, let alone this kind of generosity.

"We all look out for each other here in Lilac Ridge," Melody cooed. While that might be the case now, it hadn't always been. Everyone bowed to whatever the Hale's wanted, and since the scandal with Jill's family had likely disrupted the peaceful climate here, Jill had expected the town to hate her.

41

"How long have you lived here?" Jill asked.

"Two years. I started out as an event coordinator at Austin's first resort in Vale. He liked my work so much he brought me on as the event manager at his second resort in Hawaii. I've pretty much followed him from resort to resort."

"Then how'd you end up here?" Austin only recently moved back, as far as she knew. Had she known he was here, Jill may have considered simply selling the Barn or homing the animals and shutting it down, just to avoid him.

"I guess you could say my biological clock kicked in. I got tired of moving every couple years, so when the position opened here, I snatched it up. I love this little town."

~~~

A bell sounded from Melody Starr's phone. "Oh, I'm sorry. I haven an appointment with Austin. I hate to make him wait. Call me if you have any questions. Otherwise, just leave all the details to me. It'll be a perfect night, I promise."

As Melody opened the hardwood door, Jill was anxious to make her exit before Austin showed up, but when she stepped through the doorway, a wall of muscle stopped her.

She looked up to find blue eyes sparkling with mischief. "Jill," he whispered, her entire body turning soft and hot. Very, very hot.

"Austin," she whispered back, wishing she could actually speak his name like a normal person. "I'm sorry, I should have been watching—"

"No apology necessary," he interrupted, his strong hands holding her arms as Jill stepped back. "What brings you to the Hale?"

"Uh, planning, event planning. Melody, I mean, not me." Well, a grasp of the English language would be useful. "Melody is planning a fund-raising event for the Barn. Your grandmother approved it."

Austin continued to smile, as if amused by Jill's stammering. Because, of course, he already knew all this.

"I need to go." She shrugged out of his hold and brushed by him. As she heard him tell Melody he'd be with her in a minute, Jill stepped up her pace.

She made it outside, but not quite to her car when she felt more than heard Austin behind her. "How long before you stop running away from me?" he asked as he came up beside her.

"I'm not," she lied, turning to face him. "You're busy, I'm busy." She stopped rambling before she sounded like more of an idiot.

"Jilly," he pleaded. His hand slid around her neck, his fingers weaving into her hair and angling her head up, as if he intended to kiss her again.

It had been days since that last kiss and it still had her off-balance.

"It's Jill," she said in an attempt to dissuade him from doing just that. "Only my friends call me Jilly."

It was a brutal stab, one that worked given the pain flashing in his eyes. Maybe it made her a bitch, but she felt like she'd scored a victory.

The victory was short-lived as he pulled his hand away and stepped back. "I'm sorry for hurting you, Jillian." Worse than him being presumptuous and calling her the nickname reserved for so few was the formal use of her given name. Only her parents and people who didn't know her called her that. Jill despised it. "I'm sorry for the awful things I said. If I could take it back, I would."

If only it were that easy, but words were as lethal as a sword, cutting so deep the wound could never fully heal. "You did more than just hurt me. You betrayed me. You took your father's side, a man you claimed to despise. And just like that," Jill snapped her fingers, "you were willing to buy into all of his lies and accusations."

"I was pissed," he argued. "More than pissed. I was in a rage over what had happened here," he swept his arm back and up, practically pointing at the office where her fate had been sealed. "Then Dad came home, beaten to a pulp by your father. Part of me thought he deserved it, but the other part—"

"The other part was all Hale, up on your holier-than-thou pedestal and demanding the world bow to you."

"He was my father—"

"And he was screwing my mother," Jill bellowed. "We walked in on them, Austin. That's why my father beat the shit out of him. Not because you and I had been caught together or because I'd gotten my dad fired."

She hated defending her father's actions. What he'd done to Charleston Hale wasn't right. It was downright horrifying, but he wouldn't have lost it like that if he hadn't just been fired because of her recklessness.

"No one stood up for me when your father called me a promiscuous little slut from the wrong side of the tracks. My father hung his head in shame, and you Austin, you didn't say a word."

"I didn't say a word because it would have fallen on deaf ears. I knew how to pick my battles with my father and grandfather. I kept my mouth shut because I had a plan."

"Some plan," she muttered.

"I heard you," Austin muttered back, raking a hand through his hair long hair, "with your mother. I heard her tell you that you needed to get pregnant to forever bind you to the Hales."

Jill poked him in the sternum. "You heard my mother, but before I could tell her I wasn't going to do what she wanted, you charged in and called me a desperate little whore who was never going to see a cent of your money."

Tears pooled, but she blinked them back. Jill had shed enough tears over Austin Hale to last a lifetime. She'd told him he no longer had the power to hurt her and she was determined to hold to that. She also couldn't let Austin hurt her son. If she told him about Eric now, he'd think she did exactly what her mother demanded.

"I was wrong. I was angry and reactive and a day hasn't passed when I haven't regretted saying those words to you, Jilly. You have to believe me.

"I don't have to do anything," she bit out, desperate to get away from Austin and the tidal wave of memories.

Austin sighed in defeat, but Jill didn't feel the thrill of victory. She felt defeated too, because as much as she had hoped this was all behind them, it obviously wasn't. "All I can do is apologize. If you're not willing to accept that, then I guess there's nothing more to say."

He turned and headed toward the Hale, anger rolling off his tense shoulders and fisted hands. As Jill tugged the car door open, he turned to face her once again. "I still want a dog, Jillian. I'd appreciate a home visit sooner rather than later."

~~~

Austin wished he could be stoic and reserved like his grandmother, but he was too much like the men in the Hale family, short-tempered and reactive. Austin had learned over the years that it was better to respond than react, but whether it was being back in Lilac Ridge or facing off with Jill, his instincts had him reacting with the temper he was ashamed to possess.

Walking away from Jill was his only option until he got his temper under control. Right now, Austin wanted to punch something. Anything. Preferably something he could shatter and pulverize.

But that would get him nowhere.

Instead, he returned to the Hale. He hated this resort. There wasn't a single square inch of the place that didn't hold some sort of memory of Jill. He stormed into Melody's office. "I need to reschedule. Put something on my calendar for Friday."

Before she could respond, Austin was out of the office and taking the spiral staircase two at a time to the fourth floor.

45

The main office was a mausoleum. His grandfather's large oak desk loomed in front of the corner windows that were draped in burgundy velvet. Austin hated those curtains because they taunted and teased him as a child, daring him to hide behind the thick fabric. It was too big a temptation and each time he gave in to it, his grandfather would whoop his ass.

Storming across the room, Austin tugged at them, but the iron rods were firmly mounted to the antique woodwork. As he reared away, the portrait over the fireplace grabbed his attention. While modern photography would have allowed a quick pose, Austin's grandfather was old school. He'd commissioned an artist and demanded Austin spend an entire Saturday standing there with his father and grandfather as the artist captured the three Hale men. Austin had just turned 16 and all he wanted to do was hang out at the Barn with Jilly and the dogs.

The brass plate on the ornate frame boasted 'Hale.' Austin hated the men in that picture. They represented all the things about wealth and power Austin had worked hard to avoid.

Picking up a baseball off the desk, Austin chucked it at the painting, missing by a mile and instead shattering a glass statue that stood on the mantel.

Austin hollered then, frustrated his lack of athletic ability prevented him from damaging that wretched painting while his grandfather smiled at him from beyond the grave.

"You're a son of a bitch," Austin muttered, falling into the large leather chair behind the desk and glaring at his father and grandfather in turn.

A knock at the door was followed by it creaking open. His assistant, Sadie, peeked in. "Is everything alright?" she asked.

"Perfect," he muttered. "Find someone who can take down these damn curtains and ask my grandmother if she wants that painting. Tell her if not, I'm going to burn it."

"Of course," she said, coming fully into the room with her tablet in hand. "Melody rescheduled for Friday at two, but Courtney from the Barn also called and scheduled a home visit for three o'clock. Which one do you want me to reschedule?"

Austin glanced at his watch. It hadn't been ten minutes since he walked away from Jill. He didn't believe she'd work that fast, but maybe she had called the Barn right before driving off. Somehow, that calmed Austin. Maybe he was getting through to her after all. His chest ached at seeing the hurt in her voice and seeing it in her eyes. If he stood a chance at a future with her, he needed her forgiveness.

Sadie waited. As usual, she was all business, which Austin appreciated. She'd been his assistant for almost ten years, following him all over the globe. She didn't hide her relief when he decided to set up permanent residence in Lilac Ridge. It seemed uprooting every couple years wasn't just wearing him down. "Ask Melody if she'll come to the house, then I won't have to reschedule either appointment. I'll work from there until this office is … renovated. I need a break from this." He waved his hand around and Sadie nodded in understanding. She'd been with him long enough to know of the angst among the men in his family.

"I'll get a decorator in here as soon as possible. I assume there's no limit on budget?"

Austin laughed. She knew him so well. When it came to renovating resorts, he was a budget miser. The Hale's, after all, were in the business of making money and his grandmother had taught him not to be frivolous. He rarely made exceptions, and when he did it was for very personal reasons.

"Try to keep it under a million," he joked, earning him a smirk from Sadie.

"Is there anything else I can do for you right now?" she asked.

She could get Jill on the phone and demand she forgive him, but that wouldn't be fair to Sadie and it wouldn't work on Jill. He'd only been in Lilac Ridge for a few weeks and even though he'd kept busy, he wasn't busy enough to keep the memories of Jill and the anger with his father at a reasonable distance.

"Call Noah Spencer," he said, referring to one of his Billionaire Boys Club buddies. They didn't get together often, but one of his friends was always available to blow off some steam. "If he's up for a game of poker, call the hangar and tell them to get the jet ready."

~~~

On her hands and knees, Jill scrubbed the last of the muddy footprints. "You're going to be the death of me, Buttercup," she sighed.

"Where'd she go this time?"

Jill's heart jumped out of her chest. "Cat, geez, give a girl a heart attack."

Cat laughed. "I knocked, but you were so busy ..." her words gave way to laughter as she took in the sight of Jill's clothes.

"Well, at least you're not Austin," Jill sighed, laughing at her current state as she stood.

"Austin?" Cat's sinister smile fired up Jill's temper, not so much at her friend, but at herself for caring what she looked like when her ex barged his way into her life.

"Every time he shows up, I look and smell like this."

"Classic," Jill cooed. "You never did tell me how the prodigal son looks."

He looked good. Better than good. He looked good enough to eat. Austin Hale, however, was like carbs for a diabetic. He'd send Jill's body into a tailspin she might not be able to recover from.

"He looks the same," she shrugged, which was somewhat true. He'd transitioned from boy to man, the good looks he'd grown into as a teen amplified by age. Austin was going to be one of those men who was like a fine wine.

She stroked Buttercup's head, earning herself a kiss from the friendly but mischievous pooch. Jill was supposed to be en route to Austin's house this very minute to do a pre-adoption visit. Formalities and all.

As she was heading out the door, Buttercup made a run for it and found a huge puddle in the dirt driveway to roll around in. Before Jill could wrangle her, the dog darted back in the house, shaking out her wet and muddy fur in the kitchen and leaving a trail of muddy paw prints all over the house. Jill had managed to get the door closed to keep Buttercup from escaping again when the dog jumped, paws on chest, and licked Jill's face with an overabundance of affection, as if rolling around in the puddles was a trip to Disney World.

Erik was gone to Six Flags for the day with Cat's cousin. Without help or a kennel for the dog, she opted to give the pooch yet another bath before cleaning up.

"I'm supposed to be doing a home visit right now."

Cat looked at Buttercup and back at Jill. "You're not giving him Buttercup?"

"Of course not. I don't want to give him any dog, but I suppose I can't let my personal feelings prevent someone from adopting." Given the calamities she'd been through with this dog in the past week, it was tempting, but when the young dog wasn't overzealous about chasing a squirrel across the meadow or rolling in puddles, she was perfect. Plus, Eric adored her. The dog slept in his small bed and when Eric was home, the two were inseparable. It felt good to give something to her son he'd always wanted. Buttercup was going to be a savior if introducing father and son didn't meet Eric's hopes and dreams.

"What are you doing right now? Are you up for a home visit?"

"You bet your ass I am. I've never been in the manor."

"He's living in the gate house," she pointed out. Jill would prefer to go to the manor, because the gate house held too many memories.

"Yes, but I heard Claudia the other day. She wants you to stop by the manor after you bless her grandson with your visit."

"I meant can you do the home visit, not do it with me. I'm already late and I have to grab a shower before I can go anywhere.

49

Look at me."

"Are you sure you're not just trying to avoid him?"

Of course she was trying to avoid him. Ever since he'd helped her wash Buttercup the other day, his parting words had been niggling their way from her head into her heart.

You have the power to hurt me, Jilly.

She didn't want that power. For years she thought revenge for what he'd done to her seemed like the only thing that would put it behind her, but even keeping him from adopting a dog wasn't as gratifying as she'd hoped.

After their fight the other day at the Hale, Jill just thought she was being unreasonable.

I just hope you'll give me a chance to prove I am not my father's son.

Austin had never been his father's son, which was why his words so long ago had been such a shock to her, and why they'd cut so deep. She trusted him, loved him, and in return he threw that love and trust back in her face.

Just spending a few minutes with him while washing Buttercup sparked all those feelings Jill thought she'd put behind her. She tried to chalk it up to nostalgia, the two of them working in the Barn, taking care of the animals, commiserating over their uncaring parents. The whole town thought Austin had it all because his family was so rich, but he was just a normal kid, his family suffering the same dysfunctions as everyone else's.

"Being near him makes me nervous and angry," she admitted because Cat was her best friend and already knew the truth. "He apologized and asked me to forgive him. Do you think it's unreasonable to keep carrying this grudge or do you think I'm justified?"

"I guess you have to ask yourself why you're still carrying the grudge. Is it because of what Austin said to you or is it because of how your parents treated you?"

"You should have become a therapist instead of a marketing

goddess," Jill pointed out. It was in her nature to avoid all conversations that drew out the angst toward her parents, but if she was going to deal with the matter at hand, she had to talk about it. Cat was the perfect sounding board because she'd never judge Jill. "I guess Austin's easier to blame. I expected that kind of thing from my mother. I never expected it from Austin, but that day, it had all gone wrong."

"That's what happens when you try to christen every room in the Hale," Cat laughed.

Jill laughed too, because looking back, aside from the consequences, the situation was funny. It had been a joke at first, when Jill had said wouldn't it piss his father off if they had sex in every room of the vast resort. Then it'd turned into a challenge they were both committed to, until they were caught by Austin's father.

"I'm going to grab a shower. I'll go to Austin's but please promise you'll come with me. I don't want to be alone with him." Maybe with Cat there to run interference, he wouldn't bring up the past again and she could try not to remember how much she'd loved him. She could also avoid telling him about Eric just a little longer.

"I promise, as long as you promise to bring me to the manor."

They sealed the deal on a pinky promise and Jill hit the shower, trying not to let the memories of that day fifteen years ago play like a movie in her brain.

The simple truth was her parents had killed each other and Austin had betrayed her.

But the truth was never that simple.

It was rather ironic that two months after she'd left Lilac Ridge, Jill discovered she was pregnant. Austin's vengeful words played over and over in her head, as if her music app was stuck on replay. She didn't want his money and she couldn't have his love, so she had decided the baby was hers to raise.

Austin hadn't been fair to her. In fact, he'd been cruel, but so much had happened that day. Her world had fallen apart and knowing the compassionate boy he'd always been, she now imagined his had, too.

Maybe after all this time, she did need to let go of the past and forgive the man she'd once loved.

She also needed to tell him he had a son.

Chapter 5

JILL RECOGNIZED THE RED CORVETTE from the business lot at the Hale. She couldn't picture Austin driving it since he always liked big, powerful trucks. So why was the sports car in his driveway?

The question was answered when Melody came out the front door of the gate house, Austin in tow. Jealousy stabbed Jill in the gut, a foolish thing since she had no claim to it. She hadn't been with Austin for a decade and a half. Just because they'd shared a kiss didn't mean he wanted to be with her. It was just a tactic to get her to forgive him.

That was fine. At least that's what she told herself.

Austin's easy smile became guarded when he spotted Jill and Cat in the driveway. "Thanks, Melody," he said as the event's manager made her way to the corvette. It seemed like an expensive car for someone in her role. Had Austin given it to her?

Melody said hello as she breezed by them, way too much bounce in her step. Austin was barefoot, dressed in worn jeans and a white t-shirt. He looked delicious, as tasty as salty potato chips dipped in chocolate.

"He so does not look the same," Cat muttered as they made their way to the house, Buttercup darting ahead of them and jumping on Austin. Cat was right. His hair was longer, his shoulders wider, his hips narrower. He looked more surfer god than billionaire resort mogul, but then he'd never looked the billionaire part. Except for that one incident, he'd never acted the part either.

"Welcome, ladies," Austin greeted them after he got Buttercup settled down. "I didn't realize it took two to do a pre-adoption home visit."

"Cat volunteers at the Barn," Jill lied, although Cat had been spending plenty of time helping while Jill got acclimated to the business. "I thought it would be best if we had more than one person experienced in home visits."

Not that Cat had any experience. Neither did Jill, but she had a clipboard and a checklist and that was as good as gold as far as she was concerned. A checklist would keep her on task and hopefully prevent her from remembering all the time she'd spent with Austin in this house.

"Can I get either of you a coffee? Maybe tea?"

"I'll have a coffee, thanks," Cat said.

"No thanks, this isn't a social call," Jill said, nudging Cat with her elbow.

Austin's smile faded. "So this is how it's going to be?" he asked.

Jill sighed. She wasn't being fair. Austin was making an effort. He'd apologized, but more than that, enough time had passed that what happened shouldn't matter. Holding a grudge was a trait she'd inherited from her mother. It was time to let it go.

"I'm sorry. Yes, coffee would be great."

Austin's smile was back, the dimple in his chin forming into a crevice that could pull a girl in and keep her hostage. "Make yourselves comfortable. I'll be back in a minute."

The gate house was modest compared to the manor, but that didn't mean it was small. Outside, the three thousand square foot ranch looked like it belonged on a hillside in Tuscany. Inside, the spacious living area looked the same as it had 15 years ago, with leather furniture and dark oak bookshelves. There was a recreation room with a pool table and dartboard down one hall, along with two large bedrooms. At the opposite end of the house was the master bedroom. The galley style kitchen was at the back of the house, with a formal dining room on one side and a more casual dining area on the other.

The leather creaked as Jill and Cat sat on the couch. "This place is amazing. I can't even imagine how glamorous the manor must be," Cat cooed. "And you've had sex in every room of this house?"

"Shush," Jill said, not wanting Austin to hear.

"She has had sex in every room of this house," Austin said as he returned to the living room, a proud smile on his face and a serving tray in his hands, and Buttercup the traitor at his side.

Cat giggled as Jill blushed. Austin set the try on the table and took a seat in the adjacent chair, Buttercup jumping onto his lap. "I want the grand tour," Cat demanded after she'd grabbed a cup of coffee.

"Feel free to explore," Austin invited. "Jill and I will get down to business."

"What?" Jill bit out.

"The application? To adopt a dog? I'm sure you have questions, right? Unless you have other business you want to get down to. I'm game."

Jill blushed some more. "Right, the questions. Of course," she said, ignoring his other suggestive comments even though her body temperature had reached volcanic proportions. With Austin smiling at her, she knew he was playing a memory in his mind. It may or may not be the same one she was playing.

The first time they'd made love was right here in the gate house. They'd started out on the couch, watching a movie and eating Chinese takeout. Before the movie had finished, they were making out on the couch like the teenagers they were. He'd looked at her, the question in his eyes, and she smiled her silent answer. He led her to the bedroom, telling her their first time was going to be special. She was so nervous she was shaking, but they'd managed to undress each other. It was awkward but still magical. After that first time, their sex life exploded. They did it anywhere and everywhere and as often as they could. Jill had even gone on the Pill so they could stop using condoms.

"I know what you're thinking about," he said.

"I'm thinking we need to get to these questions," she said and focused on her list. "Where will the dog spend his or her time while in the house?" she asked.

Austin's mouth twitched with what she knew was amusement. Yes, she was still avoiding him. Being here was more overwhelming than she'd imagined, but she had a task to complete and that would get her through the next twenty minutes.

"If the dog requires a crate, I'll get one, but I intend to let him or her have free roam. I'm not opposed to a dog on the furniture or sleeping in my bed. Unless, of course, the bed is otherwise occupied."

"So you do have a girlfriend," she said before cringing. It wasn't a question on her checklist, but it was one that had been winding its way around her brain ever since she'd spotted the corvette in his driveway.

"No girlfriend," he said and took a long sip of his coffee, watching her the entire time. "How about you?"

"I don't have a girlfriend either," she said, making fake notes on the paper.

"That's too bad. Every man's fantasy."

Jill laughed and tossed the clipboard on the table, ready to abandon this whole home visit thing and find out why he was in Lilac Ridge. That's when Cat bounded back into the living room.

"This place is amazeballs. Seriously, if Jilly isn't going to forgive you, I'll be your girlfriend. I would love to live here."

"Cat!" Jill squealed.

"What? Come on. That's why you're making him jump through hoops, just so you can get more information about him. Don't be dumb, Jilly, we all know what you're about."

Jill was going to kill Cat. The best friend wasn't supposed to expose her secrets.

"Ask me anything," Austin said, leaning back in the chair, his arms stretched over the back cushions and his ankle resting on the opposite knee. Buttercup stretched, angling her head to rest on Austin's chest. He was the poster child for relaxed and Jill wished she could have just a little of that.

"I think it's best if we stick with the home visit questions."

Cat's phone beeped with a text message. She scooped it out of her purse and commenced to swearing. "I forgot about an appointment. Sorry, Jilly, but I have to run. Austin, do you think you can bring her home when you're all done here?"

Cat was already heading to the door as Austin's smile widened. "It'd be my pleasure."

Before Jill could put up a fight, Cat was gone. Jill stood to follow her out, but Austin rushed to the door and blocked her path. "I won't bite, Jill, I promise."

Well, damn, because she kind of wanted him to bite.

No, no, this was business. While she was willing to forgive the past, she wasn't sure she was ready to dive head first into the deep end of Austin Hale's swimming pool.

Speaking of. "The swimming pool is a hazard. How do you plan to keep a dog from drowning?" she asked.

~~~

As Buttercup snored loud enough to sound like a chainsaw, Austin suffered through all of Jill's adoption questions, though suffer wasn't how he'd describe it. He was amused by the whole situation. He had gained some ground and he was grateful Cat had abandoned her friend. He owed that woman big time.

"I've been marinating wings all day. You want to stay for dinner?" he asked, as if it was no big deal she was stranded at his house and he was making one of her favorite foods.

"You're not going to take me home, are you?" she huffed.

"I'm not holding you hostage," he admitted, though he'd like to keep her here forever. "If you want to go home, I'll take you home. But I made potato salad."

She sighed and he knew he had her. Jill couldn't say no to anything made with potatoes. "What about coleslaw?" she asked.

"You can't have wings without coleslaw," he said in victory.

"I haven't had a real meal in three weeks," she said, following him into the kitchen and climbing on a bar stool at the breakfast bar.

"Three weeks?" he inquired.

"Since I left Denver. I haven't had much time to cook."

He laughed. "So you do cook? You're not living on potato chips and frozen dinners?"

Her laughter pierced his heart. "Actually, I had a roommate who liked to cook. He wouldn't let me set foot in the kitchen for fear I'd burn down the house."

"Roommate?" he asked. A he, no less.

"Tony. He's gay, by the way."

"Oh, great. That's great." He assumed she was telling him she didn't have a boyfriend, but it wasn't clear in his mind. While Austin had learned to be direct in his resort ventures, Jill had him flummoxed. "Is there a boyfriend joining you in Lilac Ridge?"

Jill laughed. "Took you long enough. No, there's no boyfriend, but that doesn't mean I'm looking for one either."

She was still keeping that wall around her, but Austin felt like he'd melted the ice a little.

Austin pulled the wings from the fridge. "Tell me about your life, Jill. What have you been doing all these years?" He hoped it wouldn't send her running, but he wanted to know.

As he placed the wings on a baking sheet, Jill gave him what he knew was the short version. "That night I got in my car and drove. I didn't stop until I hit the Rocky Mountains. I've been living in Denver ever since."

Colorado. Funny that had been the location of his first resort. "You were planning to go to Northeastern University."

"I withdrew."

She cut her words short and he couldn't blame her. That night had been a nightmare. Not only had his father been cruel and Austin been worse, but her parents had killed each other.

He wanted to take it all back, to be a little less reckless so his father wouldn't have caught them in the guest room. It was Austin's fault. The rift between he and his father was well in place, and being reckless like that was a sure fire way to bring out Charleston's temper. Charleston knew how much Austin loved Jill. Even though his father time and again had forbidden Austin to see her, Austin kept at it because he was all in, heart and soul. Jill had always been the one for him and his father's insistence that he find a woman worthy of the Hale name and fortune only pushed him closer to Jill. She was worthy. Where she lived didn't matter to Austin.

Charleston had fired Jill's dad to punish Austin. That's probably why he was screwing Jill's mother too. Charleston wanted to get caught that day. Jill's dad had always been a bit of a pushover so it would have shocked Charleston that the man had a temper and unleashed it on him.

And then on Jill's mother.

Austin couldn't change the past, but he could do something about the future.

"I was going there to rescue you," he admitted. "That was my plan. I was going to take you far away from Lilac Ridge and marry you." Because his grandmother had always preached that he needed to marry for love and he knew Jill was the only one he would ever love.

Jill's eyes widened before she laughed. "You were not!"

He drew a cross over his heart. "I swear to you, Jilly, that's why I showed up at the Barn. I knew you'd go there. I packed up my clothes, stole money out of my father's safe, and headed over to get you. We had talked about Colorado, about seeing the mountains. Do you remember?"

"Of course I remember. I remember everything." A tear formed at the corner of her eye. Austin crossed the space, cupping her cheek and wiping the tear when it fell.

Her sadness broke his heart, but he didn't know how to fix the past. All Austin could do was kiss her.

Chapter 6

JILL WANTED TO FORGET. SHE'D wanted to forget the awful things Charleston Hale had said. She wanted to forget her parents' tragedy. Most of all, she wanted to forget that Austin ever hurt her.

With his lips on hers, and his hands moving down her back and pulling her closer, it was easy to forget.

It was like it'd always been, just the two of them, ignoring the fact she was from a lower class family and he was from money, forgetting they weren't supposed to love each other.

His lips were soft and strong and when his tongue slid across her bottom lip, she opened to him, wanting more, needing him to take this as far they could go.

What started out as a tentative connection exploded. Jill clung to his shoulders, practically climbing his rugged body.

His groan was like a fan over a flame, setting her on fire. He pressed her against the door and she absorbed his body heat, moaning a little herself as his erection pressed against her belly and his tongue tangled with hers.

The oven beeped and Austin released her mouth with a groan.

"Ignore it," she pleaded.

"You have no idea how much I want to," he said, yet he stepped back, his fingers trailing down her arm.

He moved across the kitchen, tugging open the oven and pulling the pan of wings out. He dropped the pan on the stove and turned back, the hunger in his eyes still sparkling.

For Jill, doubt had set in. Getting close to Austin would only stir up the past and Jill had that locked down tight, right where she needed it to be. She hadn't survived all these years by looking back. Her motto was to keep moving forward. Sissy had accused Jill of running away, but she didn't have to survive everything Jill had endured that fateful night.

"We should eat," Jill said, nodding at the chicken.

Austin ignored her suggestion and crossed the room, moving between her legs and lifting her chin until she was forced to meet his gaze. "Don't run from me."

She wasn't. Ok, maybe she was, but she needed to take a breath. Being with Austin had always been like being caught in the middle of a storm. When they were teenagers, it was exciting, even enticing, because aside from Sissy and Cat, he was the only person who didn't ignore her or make her feel like she didn't belong.

While she wanted to forgive him, it wasn't a switch she could flip. She'd been nursing her wounds for a damn long time and just because he looked at her like this and kissed her like that didn't make the scars disappear.

"I'm not going anywhere," she said in compromise. Not that she could. Cat had left her stranded at Austin's house. While she could walk the four miles, she was pretty sure Austin wouldn't let her. If Eric was home, she'd figure out a way to get there, but she wasn't expecting him back until well after the amusement park closed. The thought of being alone with her thoughts – her regret – was enough to keep her feet firmly planted.

He kissed the tip of her nose and stepped back, holding her gaze for a few more seconds, as if he needed to confirm she wasn't going to bolt. When he seemed satisfied, he went to the fridge and pulled out the potato salad and coleslaw. "Let's eat at the table," he said, moving to the informal dining area in the kitchen.

"How can I help?" she asked.

"Grab a couple beers. I'll take care of everything else."

Jill grabbed and opened the beers while Austin made quick work of getting the table set. In a matter of minutes, they were gorging on wings, Buttercup sitting with perfect begging posture just a few feet away.

It was like she hadn't eaten in weeks, and maybe she hadn't. Austin gave her a curious look when she heaped the potato salad on her plate and laughed after she'd devoured it and slapped another heap down.

If she was this famished, she couldn't even imagine how Eric must feel with his Mach ten metabolism. They'd gone from gourmet meals thanks to Tony to frozen dinners thanks to Jill's inability to pull a meal together.

"I'm going to have to make it a priority to feed you more often," he chuckled.

When Jill eased up on the indulge-fest, she licked the sauce off a finger and noticed Austin immediately went still.

Maybe the beer had calmed her nerves or she was slipping into a food coma, but the doubts that'd crept in when the oven timer had gone off were gone now. She slipped a finger into her mouth and sucked the sauce from it, earning a growl in response. On the next finger, Austin tossed the wing he'd been clinging to onto his plate and leaned back to watch the show.

"Men are so easy," Jill laughed.

"And you are so hot." His voice was thick with the gravel of desire and her body responded in kind, getting all hot and heavy and damp in the right places.

When she finished cleaning her fingers, she went to the sink and washed her hands, grabbing a couple more beers on the way back.

Austin still had that ferocious hunger in his eyes. "You missed a spot," he said and leaned across the table, wiping at the corner of her mouth and pushing his finger inside.

Jill obliged the invasion by sucking his finger, circling her tongue around it. "You're killing me," he groaned.

Smiling, she released his finger. "You look very much alive to me."

"Yeah, but if I don't get inside you soon and make you scream my name as you come, I might just die."

He'd never been so candid. The last time they were together, they were young, still learning. A lifetime had passed, and with it Austin had gained experience, if the tabloids were to be believed, and confidence.

"I'm right here," Jill said, trying to sound as confident.

Austin stood and pulled Jill out of her chair and against him. His mouth claimed hers in a rough kiss that left no doubt as to his intentions.

Backing her against the wall, he slipped his fingers between hers and raised her arms over her head, bringing their bodies flush from chest to thigh. Her hard and needy nipples pushed against her bra, begging to be released and ravaged as heat pooled between her thighs.

Now he was the one killing her.

Austin released her mouth and she tried to catch her breath as he trailed kisses across her jaw.

"You smell so good," he whispered against her ear.

"Don't stop, Austin," she pleaded. "Please don't stop."

He stepped back, his piercing blue eyes making her want, need. "I promise, Jilly. I won't ever stop unless you want me to."

"Make me forget," she pleaded, nearly ripping her shirt off and tossing it on the floor.

Austin's smile widened. "I intend to make you remember."

Scooping her up in his arms, Jill laughed, loving his strength. He told Buttercup to stay in the living room and moved with purpose to the bedroom, kicking the door closed and placing her on the large bed.

"You're wearing far too many clothes," she pointed out, raising her brow. While he looked fantastic in the worn jeans and t-shirt, she wanted him naked before she could think about what they were doing and come to her senses.

"My clothes are fine. For now." The sparkle was back in his eyes as they moved over her body, leaving a hot trail in their midst. "Yours, though, need to go."

He leaned over her on the bed, one arm landing next to her shoulder, bracing his body above her. He traced her lips with his finger, causing a tingle that inspired her to lick her lips.

"I thought," she paused because it wasn't her style to verbalize anything sexual, but maybe that needed to change. "I thought you needed to get inside me and make me scream your name?"

Fire seemed to ignite in his eyes, his chest rising and falling like he was struggling to breathe.

"I'm going to make you scream my name," he growled, "more than once."

Chapter 7

It had been a long time since a man had touched her, and even then, it had never been like this.

Austin moved slowly, methodically, opening her jeans and caressing the skin above her panty line with the tip of his finger. It tickled, but at the same time sent a rush of desire under her panties.

She couldn't wait, so she lifted her butt and pushed her pants down. Austin chuckled, that sexy smile making her want everything it promised.

Pushing herself up, Jill moved her hand around his nape and pulled him to her. His mouth was hot and demanding as he reached behind her with one hand and released her bra. She chuckled because he'd practice that move countless times when they were younger, but he'd never manage to master it.

"You've been practicing," she said against his mouth. It didn't bother Jill that he'd been with other women, at least not now. Together they'd shared their first kiss and later lost their virginity together. Those were things all those supermodel women would never have.

"I've fantasized about this, with you. It was always so perfect with us, but I've wondered what it would be like to make love to the woman, not the girl."

It had been perfect, right up until the night when their world fell apart. Jill didn't want to think about the past. She wanted Austin, here and now. Maybe it was selfish because she knew it was all going to fall apart again, but she needed this one moment with him.

He massaged her breasts, his thumbs brushing across her nipples and sending a surge straight to her core. When his mouth found one nipple, she fell back on the bed, losing herself in the pleasure of his erotic kiss. His long, loose hair added to the erotic touch and she couldn't resist weaving her fingers into it and holding him right where he was.

Austin had other plans, though. After lavishing her other nipple, he kissed a straight line down her belly until he reached the border of her panties. He teased with his fingertips, back and forth along the edge of the seam, then sliding his fingers beneath the seam, but not going any further.

Jill thought she was going to explode with the need for him to touch her. It seemed like a lifetime of pleasure and desperation before he eased the panties down her thighs.

He kissed her thigh and hip before whispering something that sounded like "I've missed you." Then his mouth was on her and the sentiment was lost. Her hips thrust off the bed, demanding more of his kiss and Austin obliged, his tongue sweeping across her center before pushing inside her. She cried out from the pleasure and felt the pressure of his arms holding her hips to the bed. The scrape of his stubble-roughened chin was in such contrast to his soft and warm mouth that it pushed Jill to the edge. Then he found her clit and she was calling his name as the orgasm rushed through her, clenching her fists and curling her toes.

When the tremors subsided, Austin kissed her hip and across her belly, meandering his way up her body until he lavished her sensitive nipples again. Then he stopped and she opened her eyes find him smiling.

"You're still wearing too many clothes," she pointed out, brushing her bare leg against the denim covering his.

"Remember the first time I went down on you? I came in my pants."

She did remember. She'd wanted to give him as much pleasure as he'd given her, but when she tried to open his jeans, he had stopped her. He'd been embarrassed but Jill was flattered that giving her pleasure had gotten him off too.

"Did you this time?" she asked, moving her hand over the abundant bulge in his jeans.

Austin pushed up, kneeling between her legs and opening his jeans, proving he hadn't gone all teenage boy on her this time.

After moving off the bed, he stripped out of the jeans and grabbed a condom out of the drawer. He didn't give Jill the chance to put it on him. By the time he was back on the bed, he was moving over her and pushing her legs open with his thighs.

He had a look in his eyes like he wanted to say something. Jill held her breath because she knew what words lingered between them, even as just a memory.

Every time they had made love, just before he pushed inside her, Austin always told her he loved her.

He couldn't love her now. Time and distance. Heartache and tragedy. It had all changed them. Austin the man was much like the boy she'd loved, but Jill was different. She had secrets that would destroy even the glimmer of hope between them before it had a chance to spark into something more.

"You're so beautiful," he said and the hope faded. Jill wasn't sure what she would have said if he'd claimed to love her, but deep in her heart, she'd wanted to hear the words.

Even with the hope gone, she still had the man here, wanting her and she'd take that knowing it was all she could ever have of him. "Make love to me," she whispered.

Austin's lips brushed hers as he rubbed himself up and down the center of her before pushing in. He was thick and hot and Jill moaned from the pleasure of being filled by him.

"So beautiful," he whispered across her ear, his breath warm and arousing on her neck.

He moved slowly and pushed deep. The contact had her skin tingling and wanting more. She lifted her knees, bringing them next to Austin's hips and he hooked an arm under one to bring it even higher.

"Oh, God," he groaned as he pushed deeper.

They moved together, Austin kissing her neck and then her mouth and then her neck again. Her release teased, the tingle starting right at her core and cascading out. Jill thrust her hips with more urgency, her own pleasured moans matching Austin's.

She hadn't felt like this in so long. Austin had always had a way of making her just feel and Jill hadn't realized how numb she had felt.

Releasing her knee, Austin moved her arms over her head, his fingers locking with hers. She wrapped her legs around his, connecting them from fingers to toes. His skin was hot, the light spray of hair on his chest teasing her nipples.

"Jilly," he whispered across her ear. "Come for me."

She'd never been one to do anything on command, but her body obeyed Austin without question, the tingle exploding in an array of pleasure that had her crying his name before her breath caught in the midst.

As her body tightened around him, he grunted her name with his release.

The intensity faded as Austin stilled on top of her. He kissed her neck, releasing her arms and trailing his fingers down her arms and torso.

"You are so beautiful," he said as his blue eyes held hers captive.

She brushed the hair from his face and smiled, hanging onto the moment for as long as she could. It was selfish not to tell him her secret, but her inner coward prevailed as she moved her hand to his nape and pulled him to her for one last kiss.

~~~

Jill sat bolt upright, her breath locked tight in her chest and sweat beading on her forehead.

She'd been back there, at the fire, watching her house go up in flames. In the smoke were whispers, hateful words that she wished were just part of the nightmare, but they weren't. The words were real. They'd been spoken and they'd cut her deep.

She'd opted to forgive the man who spoke them, but he wasn't the only one who had said them. He wasn't the only one who had hurt her that night.

Haunted by the memories, she slid out of bed as quietly as possible, picking up her scattered clothes as she moved across the room. She dressed only after she'd left Austin's bedroom, then made for the living room and her purse.

It was dark, almost ten according to the digital clock next to Austin's bed. Cat's cousin would be bringing Eric home soon and Jill needed to be there. Since Cat had abandoned Jill, she damn well could get back here and take Jill home.

Jill stopped short as she reached the living room. It looked like a fabric store had exploded, foam and leather everywhere. Off-white foam covered the floor in small pieces, making Jill feel like she was inside a snow globe that had settled after being shaken. A mass of golden fur was curled into a ball in the middle, as if Buttercup had built herself a nest.

The growl that vibrated in Jill's chest woke the dog, who wagged her tail and got that "oh-my-god-I'm-so-happy-to-see-you" look in her face before she bolted to her feet and jumped on Jill.

"Naughty girl," Jill chastised, taking in the mess. Oh, God, she hoped the dog hadn't eaten her phone. She remembered she'd left it in the kitchen, where things with Austin had gone from comfortable to out of control in 2.1 seconds.

When she came out of the kitchen, scrolling to find Cat in the contacts, she ran right into the solid wall of Austin.

"Oh," she cried as he smiled down at her.

"Running away again?"

Before she could answer, his mouth was on hers, making her want to do anything but run away. Her toes curled against the hardwood floor as she wrapped her arms around his neck and pulled herself closer.

Jill forced herself back to reality before she lost herself in his touch again. "I have to go."

"Spend the night with me," Austin said, his hand brushing her cheek.

She couldn't, not without telling him about Eric and she was sure if she told him about Eric, he not only wouldn't want her to spend the night, but he wouldn't want her at all. She needed to tell him, but she needed a solid plan first.

"Buttercup destroyed your couch," she pointed out.

The dog sat on the floor next to them, eliciting a head scratch from Austin. "This furniture is old and musty. She did me a favor, now I have an excuse to replace it."

"Don't give her the impression this is ok. I can't afford to replace the furniture at Sissy's." The last thing Jill needed was the dog tearing up Sissy's couch. Fortunately, the cats hadn't done too much damage to it.

She stepped away and got back to finding Cat in her contacts.

"Who are you calling?" Austin asked.

"Cat. I told you, I need to go. She can come get me."

He placed his hand over the phone. Jill was about to protest when he said, "If you won't stay, I'll take you home."

While Austin dressed, Jill sent a text to Eric. He responded immediately, saying they were still on the road but were almost back in Lilac Ridge.

She needed to get moving. She went to the kitchen to grab a

trash bag and returned to the living room to find Buttercup sweeping the couch debris back and forth with the wag of her tale.

"I can't believe you did this," Jill chastised. Buttercup didn't seem at all bothered as she continued to wag her tail and smile.

When Austin came back, fully clothed this time, he crept down and helped Jill clean up the mess. "Thanks," he said when they got the bulk of the torn up padding and fabric into the garbage bag. "You didn't have to do that."

"She's my dog. I'm responsible. I should buy you a new couch too—"

"But you're not going to."

She knew he wouldn't let her and knowing how wealthy he was and how short on cash she was, it wasn't an argument she was going to pursue.

"I'm ready to go," she insisted, knowing she didn't have a lot of time before Eric got home. She didn't want to explain why she was coming home so late, with Austin, of all people, bringing her home.

She shouldn't have given in to her desire, but it had been so long since anyone had looked at her the way Austin did, and touched her the way he did.

After getting Buttercup into the back seat of the F150, Jill climbed in the front. The truck smelled new, and she supposed it had to be if Austin had just returned to Lilac Ridge from a decade and a half of travels.

"Why did you move back?" she asked as he got the truck moving. "You've been opening a new resort every couple years. Don't you like traveling the world?"

He gave her a quick glance, the corner of his mouth turned up in a smirk. "Been keeping tabs on me?"

She didn't want to admit to that, so she just turned and looked out the window. There wasn't much to see. Austin lived at the northern tip of Lilac Ridge. It was a narrow and winding road that led back to town.

"Nana asked me to come back. She came to see me a few

months ago and said it was a dying woman's last wish that I come home and settle down, start a family. I thought she was dying, so I came back."

Jill gasped. Claudia had looked so healthy, had even said she hoped she had many years left. "I'm so sorry, Austin, I didn't know."

"No, it's fine. She's fine. It wasn't her dying wish, it was Sissy's. I think Sissy was trying to reunite us. She knew she was dying, that you would come back here to run the rescue."

"I–" Jill started, but what could she say? Dammit, Sissy. She had never liked that Jill didn't tell Austin about Eric, but she'd agreed to keep the secret.

"The truth is I was ready. I've been ready for a while. Traveling has been great, but Lilac Ridge has always been home." He smiled and put his hand on hers, giving it a gentle squeeze. "More so now that you're here."

Just like the Grinch, Jill's heart grew three sizes. She didn't miss the fact this was the perfect opportunity to tell him about Eric, but that would ruin the moment. Austin would be angry. She still wasn't sure if he'd be angry she'd gotten pregnant to begin with or because she'd never told him, but she wasn't ready to walk through that door.

The truck slowed as they reached town. As they coasted over the tracks, she saw his gaze shift down Railroad Street. "Have you been down there?" he asked, his voice echoing with sympathy.

"No," she said. There was no reason to go down there. Her house had burned to the ground. The rubble had been cleaned up, and her parents' remains laid to rest in the cemetery, according to Sissy, but Jill had informed her aunt she didn't want updates.

"It's a park, with lilacs and benches and a fountain."

"What?" she said, turning to meet his gaze. "Who would do that?"

"I did. It was the first property I bought. I hated what had happened, felt responsible. I still do. So I did what I could and turned it into a park and donated it to the town. I can't believe Sissy didn't tell you."

"I wouldn't let her. Once my parents were buried, I forbid Sissy from telling me anything about Lilac Ridge and the people in it."

Austin reached over and squeezed her knee.

"I want to see you again," he said.

"That's not a good idea," Jill whispered.

"It's a great idea, Jilly. We're good together. Even after all this time, we're still good together."

"I can't be with you and not remember what happened that night, Austin. It hurts too much to have a constant reminder of everything I lost that night."

"I get it–"

"No, you don't. Your parents didn't kill each other that night. In fact, nothing changed for you. Your parents are alive, hell, they're still together. You didn't have to climb out of the proverbial ashes and start a brand new life in a place where no one labeled you a little slut from the wrong side of the tracks. You didn't lose anything."

"I lost you, Jilly. To me, that *was* everything."

Chapter 8

JILL SUCKED IN A STRANGLED breath and tried to keep the tears from falling. Austin had been so cruel that night, she'd never considered he'd been hurt in the process.

As they pulled up to her house and the porch light was on, it became very clear even through her tear-blurred vision that she was going to hurt him again.

"What the …" Austin's words tapered off as his gaze focused over Jill's shoulder.

She didn't have to turn to know what he'd seen. Eric had gotten home first.

Turning slowly, she found her son sitting on the step, the porch light illuminating him.

"Who the hell is that?" Austin growled.

Jill sucked in a deep breath as she turned to face him. She wasn't surprised to see anger seething off him. He knew who he was looking at. He may as well have been looking in a mirror.

"I was going to tell you," she whispered.

"Tell me what?"

75

Mustering her courage and remembering why she had never told Austin about Eric, she let her own pain and anger surface. "That's my son, Eric."

Austin's lip twitched, his gaze still on Eric. "Eric," he said, as if testing how the name felt crossing his lips. Austin had always hated his name. He thought it was stupid how all the Hale men were named after a city and swore any son of his wouldn't be. He'd even once mentioned 'Eric' as a good, strong name for a boy. "How old is he?"

"Fourteen."

Now his attention turned to Jill, his eyes narrowed. "And his father?"

"I think you know."

Austin gripped the steering wheel while he scowled at Jill. She'd imagined this exact situation in her head a thousand times. Maybe not in his truck in Sissy's driveway, but she knew there'd come a time when she would have to tell him. She'd had no doubts he'd be angry.

"You were pregnant," he muttered.

She didn't answer because number one, it wasn't a question, and number two, obviously she'd been pregnant. That's how babies came along.

"You were pregnant," he said, anger increasing his volume. "And you didn't think I should know?"

"I don't think this is the right time for this conversation," she responded, knowing Eric was watching, and given Austin's volume, listening.

"You're right. A right time would have been 15 damn years ago."

Austin stared over her shoulder. "Eric," he said again. "Eric Hale?"

"Eric Butler," she whispered, knowing that was pushing the knife deeper, though she wasn't sure if the stab was into his heart or his ego.

"I'm not even on the birth certificate?" he pleaded.

"No."

Buttercup whined in the back seat before a knock on the window had Jill jumping.

The door opened as she released the seat belt. "Come on, Mom," Eric said.

"Take Buttercup in the house, I'll be there in a minute," she said, giving her son a reassuring smile.

"I'm not leaving you alone with him," Eric said, his temper rivaling that of his father's.

Jill touched Eric's hand, giving it a quick squeeze. "I'm fine. Go inside, bud. Please. I promise I'll be there in just a minute."

Eric pinned his father with a stern look before opening the back door and grabbing Buttercup's leash.

He glanced back one more time after stepping onto the porch. Jill gave him a smile and a nod and he disappeared in the house.

"Does he know," he choked out, "that I'm his father?"

Jill nodded. "He's always known."

"So you've already turned him against me. I didn't even know and you've had 14 years to turn him against me."

"That's not how it happened," she said. She'd been honest with Eric from the beginning, without giving details. She hadn't defended Austin, but she had insisted Eric form his own opinions and not base his feelings off what happened so long ago.

Even though that moment still directed Jill's feelings toward him. "He's always wanted to meet you, but you made it clear what place I had in your life."

"Yeah, I guess I did. Looks like I'll be paying for that one mistake for the rest of my life."

Jill slid out of the truck, but before she closed the door, she met Austin's angry glare. "I won't let you hurt him, Austin. I won't let anyone in your family hurt him."

~~~

Austin was out of his mind.

With anger.

With regret.

It was late, but his grandmother was a night owl and he needed answers. When he stormed into the manor, he wasn't surprised to find the lights on in the conservatory. It was her favorite room.

She closed her book and looked up at him, not saying a word, and that's when it hit him.

"You knew. You knew I had a son and you didn't tell me." Did everyone know? Was Austin the only one who hadn't been privy to that little detail?

She put the book on the table and angled toward him. "It wasn't my place to tell you."

"How long have you known?" he demanded, ashamed at his Hale temper but too angry to reel it in.

"Sissy told me just before I visited you in France."

Her trip to France hadn't been planned. Nana never visited him at the resorts. She said that legacy was his and she wanted no part of it. Austin had been thrilled to see her and proud to show off what he'd accomplished. Nana had seemed truly proud.

He turned, fisting his hands. "You should have told me."

"It was my job to get you home. It was Jill's job to tell you about your son."

"Fourteen years, Nana. She kept him from me for 14 goddamn years!"

"And who could blame her, after what your father did to that poor family and after what you said to that poor girl."

Austin paced the room, his soft sneakers squeaking on the tile floor. Dammit, he wanted to break something, pick up one of the plants and toss it through the glass. That was his father's temperament, and his grandfather's. Austin had fallen prey to that temper more times than he could count, but he knew it was at least one too many. With clenched fists, he swallowed the anger and searched his soul for a way get through this without surrendering to the Hale temper.

"Did you know Sissy was engaged to your grandfather?" Nana asked, stopping Austin in his tracks.

"What?" he wasn't sure he heard that right.

"Yes, it's true. Sissy was Orlando's true love. Ironic, really, that your father had an affair with Sissy's niece. I think he sought out Caroline just to torment Orlando. Then you went and fell in love with Jillian."

"I didn't fall in love with her to torment anyone," Austin bit out. Falling in love with Jill had nothing to do with his family. It was all her. She had been his best friend, his confidant, and she'd stolen his heart. "I never should have let her go," he murmured.

"Life is too short for regrets, my dear boy. She's here now, as is your son. Is it true, that he looks just like you?"

Austin couldn't help but smile. "Spitting image," he said, pride pushing aside the anger. "He's strong, protective of Jill. God, Nana, I don't know if I can win him over."

Nana clicked her tongue as if Austin was a boy doing something he shouldn't be. "It's not about winning. You have to earn his trust. He doesn't know you."

"No, and Jill has turned him against me."

"Has she?" Nana asked.

Austin didn't know what to say. Eric's words, *I'm not leaving you alone with him*, held so much contempt.

"You have a temper, Austin. Just like your father and just like his father. You are also fiercely protective of those you love. Maybe your son inherited those traits from you."

Austin dropped into the wicker chair across from his grandmother. "They'd have to be inherited since I was never given the chance to teach him."

"You talk like it's too late. Jillian is here now. She wouldn't have come had she not intended for you to find out about the boy."

Maybe not, but she'd had plenty of opportunities to tell him since they'd both returned to Lilac Ridge.

"Why are you defending her?"

"I'm not. I lost 14 years with my great-grandson, but as a mother, I understand the need to protect a child. I raised your father Orlando's way and he turned into a person who is very difficult to like. Lucky for me, your parents were busy being selfish, affording me the opportunity to raise you the way your father should have been. Jillian was good for you, she was a good person, like Sissy, and I trust she's done a good job raising your son."

His son. Never in a million years had Austin imagined he had a son. If he'd hurt Jill so much that she felt compelled to keep their son away from Austin, could he ever find his way back into her heart? He thought he had. Their night together had been amazing. Thinking about it now, it almost seemed like good-bye.

Nana was right, who could blame her? His father was a world class prick, just like his grandfather, and Austin had acted like one too. She'd had a hard life growing up. Jill's mother was as mean and manipulative as Charleston Hale and directed all of her anger toward Jill.

Guilt ravaged him as he fell into the chair opposite his grandmother. Jill had raised their son on her own — alone — because as she'd said, Austin betrayed her with his father's accusations. He deserved to be left out of the boy's life, but Jill didn't deserve the hand she'd been dealt. He had to make things right, to show her she wasn't alone in raising their child. This, though, was foreign territory. He'd never asked for forgiveness and had no idea how to prove to Jill he deserved it, let alone the son he'd never met.

"I don't know what to do," he muttered, feeling utterly lost.

"You'll do whatever your heart tells you."

~~~

The late night visit with his grandmother helped Austin calm down and gain a little perspective. A sleepless night allowed him to come up with a plan. Now, as he stood at the door of Jill's house, he half wished no one would answer the door. What was he going to say? Would Eric even give him a chance?

Buttercup was first to the door, but it wasn't long before Eric stood there, peering at him through the glass. He opened the glass door, the screen door still separating them. "Mom's not here."

"I know," Austin admitted, pulling off his sunglasses even though it was a clear blue sky. He had seen Jill walk across the field to the Barn about twenty minutes ago. If she wasn't home, she couldn't keep him from meeting his son, but somehow Austin still felt guilty about being here without her permission. "I came to see you."

"You made her cry last night," Eric said.

"I didn't mean to hurt her. I never meant to hurt her. I just, well, dammit, I didn't know about you. It pissed – ticked me off."

"You can swear. I'm not a two year old. I'm not going to repeat it."

"I suppose not. Can I come in?" Austin asked.

Eric crossed his arms as though he was bracing for an argument. "No."

"Eric," he pleaded.

The boy dropped his arms. "I'll come out. I'm supposed to take Buttercup for a walk anyway."

He pulled the dog back and closed the door. Austin felt like an idiot standing there and hoped to hell Jill wouldn't come back from The Barn and thwart his effort to meet his son. A few minutes later, Eric and Buttercup joined Austin on the porch.

Buttercup tore down the steps, dragging Eric behind her. She sniffed around the grass for a minute, then did her business before leading them across the field. Eric reeled her in and she settled in to a steady pace.

"You're good with her," Austin told him.

"She's my first dog. We lived in a small apartment outside Denver. No room for a dog."

"Any other pets?"

Eric shook his head. "I'm trying to talk mom into letting me keep the snake Aunt Sissy has in a cage in the basement."

"You like snakes?" Austin asked, pushing through the threatening shiver.

The enthusiasm in Eric's nodding head made Austin wonder where he'd gotten it from. Jill feared snakes as much as Austin did.

"I named him Mr. Slither. He's a king snake. I've been doing a lot of reading about them and even got him to let me hold him. Don't tell Mom though. She'd freak if she knew I had him out of the cage."

Austin was ready to freak too, but he didn't want to lose cool points this early in their relationship. "Your secret is safe with me. So did you like it there? In Denver?" It was a place Austin and Jill had talked about visiting, maybe even living there after they both finished college.

"Eh, it was alright. This is better though," Eric said, moving his arm to signal the property Jill now owned. "Well, it will be now that I can–"

His words cut off, but Austin wasn't going to let it slide. "Now that you can what?"

Eric shrugged "Do more things. I miss my friends and haven't been able to meet anyone here."

"Why not?" Austin asked. The kid seemed pretty personable. He wasn't awkward the way Austin had been at his age. Making new friends should be easy.

"Just 'cause," he muttered, stepping it out.

Austin picked up his pace and came up next to Eric. "She didn't want anyone seeing you, right? Because of me?" Looking at Eric was like looking at a younger version of himself, except his son was a lot taller and thinner than Austin had been at fourteen.

"I promised Mom I'd stay in stealth mode, be all Ninja and stuff. You know, just until she broke the news to you." Eric stopped and pinned Austin with a look that was like looking in a mirror when he was pissed off. "You have no right to be mad at her," Eric snapped.

"So she told you … what happened all those years ago?"

Eric shrugged again. Seemed to be the kid's favorite gesture. "Not really. She said her parents died in a fire and you two had a fight — that she realized she didn't know you at all."

Austin didn't know himself that night. "She didn't tell you what I said to her?"

Eric's expression changed from angry to curious and skeptical. "What *did* you say to her?"

There was no way Austin could tell him, because he couldn't say the words. They'd left a bad taste in his mouth the one time he'd uttered them, and left a gaping hole in his chest overflowing with regret.

"I said something hurtful that I've always regretted. I loved your mother. I still do." It was a declaration he hadn't expected to make, but it came from his heart. "I want to prove to her, and to you, that I'm not who she thinks I am. I want a chance to be your father."

"It was always my choice. She didn't keep me away from you. She gave me the choice whether or not to meet you."

"And you didn't want to because you didn't want me to hurt her again."

Eric nodded.

This kid was mature beyond his years. Austin hoped he'd had a chance to just be a kid.

"I promise, Eric. I promise I won't hurt her, or you." Austin held out his hand and Eric took it. He had a firm handshake for a fourteen year old and even though Austin hadn't taught him the importance of a handshake, it made him proud.

There was so much more to say, but Austin didn't want to

overwhelm his son during their first meeting, nor did he want to push him away, so they walked across the field in silence for a while before Eric spoke up.

"I follow you, you know, online. About your resorts and stuff."

"Oh yeah?" Austin asked, surprised and pleased by the declaration.

"Yeah. It's cool, all those buildings you've saved. You make a lot of money doing that?" Eric asked.

"Eventually, yes. It's an investment, at first. A risk, but I guess that's what I like about it. There's no reward if there's no risk."

"I like to build things too. It started with Legos and then I got into models. I think I'd like to go into construction. Maybe be an engineer."

That's how Austin had started out, too. "I'm looking at an old resort in Nova Scotia," Austin admitted. He hadn't committed to it yet, but it was close enough that he could manage the project from Lilac Ridge, especially once the new headquarters was established here. "Maybe I could show it to you, see what you think?"

"That'd be cool," Eric said, a big smile on his face. "Does that mean I get to fly your jet?"

Austin laughed. "Yes, we'll take the jet, but we'll leave the flying to the pilot."

When they reached the wood line, they turned and headed back toward the house.

"I'm not sure where we are supposed to go from here," Austin admitted. This whole Dad thing was new to him and he didn't want to screw it up.

"I don't know either," Eric shrugged. "I don't even know what to call you."

Asking Eric to call him Dad might be asking too much, but Austin didn't get anywhere without taking risks. "You can call me Austin, if that makes you more comfortable, but I have no objections to you calling me Dad. I know I haven't earned the name yet, but I want to."

Eric looked over at the Barn before dropping his gaze to the dog.

"Do you think that'd piss your mom off?"

"I don't know," Eric shrugged.

"We can take it slow. Just call me 'Hey You' until you're comfortable or until we have your mom's approval."

That elicited a smile from the kid. "You don't seem so bad," Eric said.

Austin laughed. "I'll take that as a compliment. So do you like to fish? Maybe I can take you. Starlight Lake has some pretty decent white perch."

"I've never been fishing. It's always something I wanted to do, but Mom doesn't eat fish and worms freak her out."

Austin remembered that. He and Jill had gone fishing several times, but he always bated the hook and handled the fish she caught. "I'll talk to her, maybe we can go this weekend."

Eric was smiling now. "Sure. I better go."

They shook hands again, but Austin couldn't stop himself from pulling the boy in for a hug. He was surprised when Eric hugged him back.

When he released the boy, Buttercup whined, asking for a little attention for herself. They both obliged.

"I'm not sure what to do about your mother," Austin said. This was foreign territory. When he was a kid, things with Jill had been easy because their love had grown so naturally. As an adult, the short relationships he had with women were easy because he knew they meant nothing.

Now, nothing was easy. Jill had become a complicated woman because of circumstance, but he couldn't let her go. He just didn't want to push her away.

"Try taking her on a date."

Could it be that simple? "I'm not sure she'd let me," Austin admitted.

"How about the fund-raiser? Isn't that a dating thing?"

Austin had heard some talk around the resort about the fund-raiser. Melody had even asked him to participate as a bachelor in the auction. Since Austin wasn't interested in dating anyone except Jill, he had declined. That didn't mean he couldn't bid on Jill, though.

"That's a brilliant idea," Austin said, patting Eric on the shoulder.

Chapter 9

JILL HAD CLIMBED TO THE loft for some perspective. As a kid, this was her escape, the place she came to think and plan and dream.

She wasn't surprised to find it exactly how she had left it fifteen years ago. Pictures she and Austin had cut out of travel magazines plastered the walls, faded now with time. The blanket they'd kept up here to cuddle on was shredded, obviously accosted by barn mice looking to make a comfortable nest.

The round loft had four small windows, all covered with dust and dirt and cobwebs. When Jill brushed her hand across one of the panes, her breath caught. Austin stood outside the kitchen door, his hands tucked into his pockets and his shoulders slumped. She wanted to race down the ladder to protect her son, but then Austin stepped back, as if to leave. But he didn't. Instead, he stood in the dirt driveway, his posture straightening as his gaze shifted to the barn and then up to the loft.

Holding her breath, she waited for him to acknowledge her, but she wasn't even sure he could see through the dingy windows. No, he couldn't know she was up there, laying more ghosts to rest.

She prayed for him to leave, but then Eric stepped out of the house with Buttercup. He nodded at his father and they stepped off toward the field.

Jill's motherly instincts screamed for her to haul ass down that ladder and tell Austin to get the hell away from her son, but she pushed it aside.

He's not going to hurt Eric, a voice deep inside her head whispered. The hurt in his voice last night had torn Jill in two. For all her excuses, Austin's regret had inspired her own. While keeping Eric from Austin had been about protecting him, it had also been about protecting Jill, more than she'd ever been willing to admit.

They disappeared from view and Jill crossed to the next window, frantically wiping at the cobwebs and dust. Their pace was slow, casual, Austin's hand still tucked in his pockets while Eric plucked the wildflowers and tall grass. Jill would give anything to be a bee buzzing around, listening to this first conversation between father and son.

Where the field ended and the woods began, they turned and strolled back. It seemed like an eternity and Jill realized when they returned that she was soaked with sweat. She should have pushed the windows open for ventilation, but she didn't want to give away her position.

After reaching the house, the two shook hands. Jill's knees gave out when the handshake turned into a hug.

Eric had gotten what he always wished for — his father in his life. Tears stung her eyes knowing she'd prevented this reunion from happening sooner. She hadn't known what to expect from Austin, and though she'd hoped he would accept his son with open arms, his family and that night when their worlds had come crashing down made it difficult to hope.

When Austin left, Eric took Buttercup back inside. Jill stood at the top of the ladder, knowing it was her only way down but fearful of the ghosts she had to face on the journey.

That night when her father snapped, Jill had come here to hide from reality. She sat in the loft for hours, hoping Austin would find her. It was only when Sissy called her that Jill climbed down. When she reached the bottom, her mother scowled at her.

Climbing down the ladder now, Jill remembered it like it was yesterday, her last interaction with her mother.

"You little bitch," her mother had cried. "Charleston was ready to leave Diana. He was going to marry me. I was finally going to have everything I've worked so hard for, but you had to be a little tramp and screw his son. You will make this right, Jillian. You will get pregnant by that boy and forever bind this family to the Hales. You owe me that."

Based on her mother's angst toward Jill and basic math, Jill suspected her parents married because Caroline had gotten pregnant. It was easy to see Caroline and Joe had never been happy. Jill's mother wanted the kind of lifestyle her father just couldn't provide. Caroline had always held it over Jill's head, blaming her for causing them to live in near-poverty instead of having the life she deserved. It was no surprise Caroline had been having an affair with Charleston Hale.

Before Jill could tell her mother to go to hell, which was exactly what she'd intended, Austin stormed into the Barn, repeated his father's words and stormed off before Jill could defend herself.

When she was finished screaming at her mother, Jill ran into the woods and only came out when dusk fell. She headed down the tracks to her house, ready to pack her things and leave for college. She was sure she could find an apartment and a job, but if not, she'd camp out until the dorms opened.

Instead of finding her house, she found smoke and flames and fire trucks. Her parents were nowhere to be found, not even after the smoke cleared. With nothing to pack, Jill had gotten into her car and driven west, stopping when she hit the Rocky Mountains and rock bottom with her emotions. When she called her aunt, Sissy informed Jill her parents had died in the fire. It sounded so innocent the way Sissy said it, but Jill knew the truth. Her parents hadn't just died in that fire, they'd killed each other.

Reaching the bottom of the ladder, Jill sucked in a deep breath. She'd survived and her mother wasn't there to torment her. She still had other ghosts to face, like visiting the park Austin had built and seeing their graves, but that would lead to the closure she'd avoided all these years.

Jill headed back to the house, desperate to see that Eric had survived meeting his father.

He sat at the counter on a barstool, reading a comic book. He smiled at her, his mouth stained orange from the cheese puffs he snacked on.

"You sharing?" she asked.

Eric peered in the bag before turning it to her. "Only because you're my favorite mom."

"Thanks," she laughed. After a few bites and endless silence despite all the crunching, she asked, "Did you take Buttercup out?"

"Yep," he grunted, still staring at the comic book.

As he reached in the bag, she set her hand on his, stopping him. "I saw Austin here."

Eric looked at the clock and then at her with a big, cheesy smile. "That was less than five minutes. I knew you had to be spying."

"I'm a mom, of course I was spying. I had to pass the Spying for Parents 101 course before you were born."

"There's no such thing," he laughed.

"There is and before you turned thirteen, I had to complete Advanced Spying, the Teen Years."

"You're making that up," he insisted.

"Nope. I have certificates and everything. I keep them in the safe with the eyes I wear in the back of my head."

It was obvious Eric didn't believe her as he stuffed his mouth with a handful of cheese puffs. "Are you mad?" he mumbled.

"Should I be? And don't answer while your mouth is full."

After he swallowed, he shrugged. "He was nice. He's going to take me fishing."

"Oh," she said, surprised. "That's good. Right? I mean, you want to go fishing, don't you? With him?"

"Yeah. Like I said, he was nice. It was kinda awkward at first, but I don't know, he's pretty cool, I guess."

He went back to his comic book, stuffing his face with more cheese puffs. Jill slid off the bar stool and grabbed a loaf of bread from the drawer. She pulled all the fixings for a turkey sandwich from the fridge and got to work before Eric finished off that bag of nasty-deliciousness.

After cutting the stacked sandwich into triangles, she pushed it across the counter. Eric smiled and dug in.

Jill didn't want to be a hard-ass, but she also didn't want to see her son hurt. She hoped Austin's intentions were noble, but the mother in her couldn't cling to that hope. "He doesn't make the rules, Eric. I know he's your father and I expect you to be respectful, but he's not in charge of you. He can't make you do anything."

"Chill, Mom. I'm not going to abandon you just because my dad is around now. I can handle it."

One thing she had learned is her son could handle anything. What tugged at her heart, though, was whether or not there was a place in Austin's life for her. She'd hurt him, he made that clear last night when he saw Eric and all the pieces came together. Jill was working to release all the ghosts haunting her, but the biggest one of all was the one she still loved. Austin had every right to hate her for keeping Eric from him, but with her wounds ripped open, she wasn't prepared to defend her actions. She needed a plan to make him understand she hadn't turned Eric against him.

~~~

The singles auction was wrapping up and none too soon. After a night on her feet, in super cute but not entirely comfortable black, strappy heels that matched her red and black dress, Jill was ready to kick the shoes off, slip into her comfy jammies, and eat a gallon of ice-cream.

Brent Daniels was the final bachelor for the auction and the bidding war between two women was slowing down. "Three hundred and fifty. Do I have 375?" the auctioneer called.

Jill was tempted to bid on him, but then she'd be bidding against Cat. Brent, better known as The Bear, was Courtney's older brother, the one afraid of snakes. He'd donated a sign to the rescue, as well as a bear carving for the silent auction. He had explained to Jill that he got his last two dogs from Sissy and wanted to help in whatever way he could, but that didn't include feeding the snakes again.

"350 going once, going twice, sold! To Cat Merriweather."

Cat's cheer echoed throughout the room. She'd had a little too much to drink, but since it was a cash bar and all proceeds benefited the rescue, Jill didn't complain.

"And that, my friends, concludes tonight's auction, but don't forget the bar is still open."

"Wait!" A voice called and the room fell silent. Everyone turned toward the door, including Jill, and found Austin standing there, dressed in a tuxedo. He'd been notably absent all night, but since he'd refused to be in the auction, Jill figured he had other commitments. "I'd like to place a bid for the auction."

He made his way through the room to the stage. "I'm afraid there's no one left to bid on," the auctioneer said into the microphone.

"I know, but I don't think the night would be complete if the owner of the Barn didn't participate in the auction. Don't you all agree?" Austin asked.

Jill's eyes widened as a burn rushed to her cheeks. The whole room cheered.

"$100," called Brent, who gave Jill a wink when she looked at him.

"$200," yelled Connor McCann, a pediatrician with five kids and whose wife had died a few years ago.

"$300," came another bid, this one from Darren Brown who owned the horse stables in town.

As the back and forth continued, Jill's gaze landed on Austin, who seemed to be enjoying the bidding war. She pinned him with a look that promised a painful, torturous death, but he only winked back.

The bidding slowed when it reach a thousand dollars. "Going once," the auctioneer said.

"Five thousand," called out Austin.

Every person in the room gasped.

"I have five thousand dollars," the auctioneer called. "Do I have six thousand?"

"Come on, Hale, you're a billionaire. You can do better than that!"

"You're right," Austin called out. "Where's Melody?"

"Here," Melody said, getting up from a seat in the corner and moving across the room with her tablet in hand.

Austin took the microphone from the auctioneer. "How much has the fund-raiser taken in tonight?"

He held the microphone in front of Melody. "Well, we don't have the tally from the bar yet, but from the dinner, silent auction, and singles auction, we're looking at roughly $9000."

"I'll match it. For a date with Jill, I'll match whatever funds are raised tonight."

"Austin," Jill warned, but he just smiled and winked.

She didn't like this. While she wanted to make peace with Austin, and maybe even pursue the spark that ignited between them after all this time, she didn't like that he thought all their problems could be solved with his money. "You can't buy my affection."

Shaking his head, Austin's smile faded, he stepped down from the stage, still speaking into the microphone. "I'm not trying to buy your affection. I'm buying a chance to prove to you I'm not Orlando Hale and I'm not Charleston Hale. I'm Austin Hale, a man who doesn't let others choose who he loves." As he stepped up to her, he dropped the microphone to his side. "I promise you, Jill, I'm not the arrogant, self-serving asshole you think I am."

Austin was never an arrogant, self-serving asshole. Just the opposite. He had always been kind and generous, if not a little insecure. Jill understood in the heat of the moment when their worlds were crashing around them, Austin said something he didn't mean — and she'd been too devastated to fight for their love.

"I don't think that," she said, wishing they didn't have the entire town watching them.

"Good. That'll make our date that much more fun." He turned his attention to the audience. "Anyone going to outbid me?"

Austin looked around the room and when he seemed satisfied no one was going to speak up, he handed the microphone to the auctioneer and raised his brow.

"Okay, we have a bid to match whatever funds are raised tonight. Going once,"

"Sold," Jill yelled.

Austin looked at her, surprise furrowing his brow.

"I want to give you a chance, Austin, but you didn't have to buy a date with me. You could have just asked."

"What? And miss my chance to be a hero? The rescue is worth it, Jilly." A spark flashed in his eyes, his hand moving around to cup her nape. "So are you."

The crowd erupted in cheers and applause as Austin pierced her heart with that blue gaze. When she thought he'd kiss her, he grabbed her hand and led her out the back door of the Hale's function room. "Our date starts now."

The moonless sky twinkled with a million tiny stars. Austin's hand was warm in hers, his grasp firm as he led her to the parking lot.

"Where are you taking me?"

"To the airport. The jet is waiting," he said.

Jet? "Austin, I can't just leave Eric."

"He's already on board and my grandmother took Buttercup.

Courtney will take care of the animals at the barn and Eric fed Mr. Slither a couple days ago, so he's all set."

Chuckling, Jill shook her head, trying to keep up with Austin who walked like he was on a mission. Given all the planning, it was obvious he was. "Awfully cocky of you, don't you think?"

He stopped and pulled her against his very warm body. "Confident, not cocky. I didn't want you to have a reason to say no."

"Austin," his name was a whisper on the cool August breeze.

"I love you, Jilly."

She opened her mouth, but Austin's fingers pressed against her lips. "Don't say anything. Just let me…" he cleared his throat and dropped his fingers. "I can broker a real estate deal without having to think about it, but being alone with you, needing to say all the right words, I'm like that pudgy little rich kid every one bullied."

"Not everyone," she reminded him.

"No, not everyone. Not you," he took her hand in his and his warmth seeped into her again. "Nana always preached that I needed to marry for love. Whenever she'd have a fight with my grandfather, or when my parents would fight, she'd tell me no matter what, I had to marry for love."

"Sissy used to say the same thing."

"When Nana came to France, and asked me to come home, to settle down, start a family, her words echoed in my mind and the only picture they conjured was you. It's always been you."

"I know," Jill confessed. "All these years, I've been so angry, and not just because of what you said. I've been angry because I didn't fight for us."

"Oh, Jilly," he said, his voice a plea before his mouth claimed hers.

When he pulled away, he reached inside his tuxedo and dropped to his knee.

"I love you, Jill. I love you and I love Eric and I want to marry you and be a family." He held out a ring that sparkled brighter than all the stars in the sky.

"I love you, Austin. Always. I've always loved you," she admitted, because despite the hateful words he'd uttered in the heat of the moment, she somehow knew they'd never been his.

"I hear a but in there," he said, looking terrified.

"I have to talk to Eric. This affects him too."

Austin smiled then. "I know. I already asked for his blessing to marry you. I promised never to hurt you, or him, and we even shook on it."

Now it was Jill's turn to smile. "You shook on it." Her son was mature beyond his years, which sometimes troubled Jill, but at times like this, it made her proud.

"The jet's ready, Jilly. We can be in Vegas tonight and married tomorrow."

She shook her head. "Vegas sounds fun, but I don't want to marry you there. Let's get married here, at the Barn." That's where everything had started. It was also where things had ended so long ago, but marrying Austin there, in the field of wildflowers felt right.

Because after all the tragedy and the years they spent apart, they were marrying for love.

Epilogue

JILL WAS MORE TOMBOY THAN pretty girl, but she loved lace and was through the roof when Austin bought her a new pair of cowgirl boots for their wedding. As she stood in front of the mirror, she couldn't believe she was actually getting married, let alone to Austin.

When she stepped into the kitchen, she found Eric. Her son was dressed in jeans, a button-down blue shirt, and a yellow tie that matched the brown-eyed Susan stuffed in his shirt pocket. He was so handsome, even more so than his father. The last fourteen years had been wonderful with him, even during the most difficult of times. Now, their family was going to be complete and Jill couldn't be more proud of the young man standing in front of her.

"You clean up good," she teased.

"I know, right? The chicks are gonna dig the new guy at school."

"The ladies," she corrected. "We don't like being referred to as chicks."

"Cat doesn't mind," Eric laughed.

"Cat's a bad influence. Any advice she offers you need to ignore."

Buttercup barked in agreement.

They both scratched the dog's ears and cooed over how smart she was before Eric looked up at Jill again. Jill straightened his tie even though it was already perfect.

"Don't crease the threads" Eric said, but still let her fuss over him. When she was done, he smirked. "So, you ready?" he asked, holding out his arm.

He was so handsome. She wasn't sure when he'd become such a mature young man, and guilt weighed on her chest knowing he'd grown up too fast because she'd raised him alone.

Jill hooked her arm through his. "I am. Are you ready? This is a big change for you too."

"He's my dad. I want us to be a family."

She wanted that too, more than anything. "I'm sorry, Eric. I should have told him a long time ago."

Eric shrugged. "You always say we have to look forward, not back. That means you can't be sorry."

Jill hugged her son. He was wise beyond his years and so forgiving. "I can still be sorry while looking forward," she told him, ruffling his hair.

"Hey, don't mess with the do. It took the perfect amount of hair gel and mad skills to get this look."

Laughing now, Jill kissed her son on the cheek. "I love you, Eric."

"Love you, too, Mom. Shall we?"

He led her out of Sissy's house and behind the barn. At the edge of the field where it dropped off to reveal an amazing view of the mountains, they'd erected a trellis for the ceremony. There Austin stood, dressed in jeans, a button-down shirt and a blue vest. While Vegas had been tempting, getting married here, behind the barn where they'd first met and where they'd spent their youth, first becoming best friends and then falling in love, was perfect.

Eric walked her down the aisle where their small group of friends and Claudia stood and when he handed her off to Austin, Eric stood beside his father as the best man.

Jill had always known Eric looked like his father, but seeing the two of them standing together, smiling the same smile and looking at her with the same blue eyes, Jill was astonished at the resemblance. Eric still looked like the boy though, with mischief in his gaze, while Austin was all man, something entirely different sparkling in his eyes.

Father and son, her men, and they were about to become a family.

Before the minister could begin, Buttercup came running across the field, her yellow coat completely covered in dark mud.

Jill thought she'd walked down the aisle with her and Eric, but she was so struck by Austin and the fact they were getting married, she hadn't realized the dog ran off.

She stopped in front of them and Jill just knew she was going to shake and spray everyone with mud. "Sit!" Austin commanded in his deep voice. To Jill's surprise, the dog complied.

"Why doesn't she listen when I tell her to do that?" she huffed.

Eric laughed and Austin smiled. "I'm the alpha, Jilly. You're just going to have to get used to that." The innuendo behind that comment was so thick Jill's knees nearly gave out.

"Stay," Austin commanded the dog a little more gently before turning back to Jill with a delicious smirk.

"Well, folks, do you want to get started?" the minister asked.

"I do," Jill and Austin said together. With that same smirk that promised a wedding night she wouldn't forget, Austin stepped forward, his mouth brushing hers as their friends cheered and clapped behind them.

They were still kissing when the minister began, "Dearly beloved, we are gathered here today …"

~   ~

Dear Reader,

I am so thrilled to bring this new romantic series to you. I can be a bit superstitious, and I've got a couple of crazy dogs, so it was fun to write this story about Jill and her superstitions, along with her love of dogs. I would love it if you would write an honest review at your preferred review site and help other readers find this and other stories. There's an unedited excerpt from *For the Love of Chocolate* and links to my other books, so keep on reading!

All the best,

Susan

Continue reading for an unedited excerpt from
For the Love of Chocolate,
the second book in the Superstitious Brides series.
This novella will be available February 2, 2015.

"You're doing it wrong."

The man's voice was a smooth caress on Maddie Carson's sweaty skin, but she ignored the heat and the words, focusing instead on the clock. Thirty-five seconds left to finish this sprint on the rower. She wasn't concerned with technique, just ... needed ... to finish.

Maddie didn't meet his gaze in the mirror, but shifted her eyes from the clock to his reflection. As usual, he didn't wear a shirt. Hot Shirtless Guy was the nickname she'd given him. It seemed tacky to work out at a fitness club without a shirt, but the view was enough to motivate Maddie to keep coming in three days a week at 5:00 in the morning, so she tried not to judge. Plus, she was fascinated by the double horseshoe tattoo on his chest. If he ever asked her why she stared at him so much, the tattoo was going to be her excuse.

Ten seconds. *No, don't put the shirt on.*

Running out of steam, Maddie finished with a few hard pulls and cooled down with a few softer pulls. "How am I doing it wrong?" she asked as Hot Shirtless Guy — unfortunately not shirtless anymore — continued to gawk at her reflection.

Why oh why did she have to wear spandex? And why wasn't her shirt ten sizes too big to hide the evidence of eating too many brownies?

"You're not pulling it back far enough. You can increase the effectiveness of the workout by pulling it back more."

Maddie did as instructed, pulling the bar all the way to her chin. Maybe proper technique would work off all that excess fat at a faster rate.

"That's too high. You want to do it lower."

She'd rather be eating a triple chocolate brownie (with milk, so it could qualify as breakfast), but that's what had gotten her into this mess, so she took the man's direction and lowered the bar. Given the way he looked, Maddie trusted he knew what he was talking about.

"Now that's too low."

Too high. Too low. Geesh, the only thing left was the in-between, and her breasts made that a challenge. How could she possibly pull the bar back with her double D's occupying all that real estate?

Raising a brow at him, he now had his lips pursed in a tight line. "You want to aim for your nipples."

As if it was an invitation, her nipples tightened and tingled, the sensation swirling around the large curves and heading south in a rush. Thank goodness for padded sports bras. Hot Shirtless Guy didn't need evidence of her silly attraction.

Maddie wasn't the obedient type, but she pulled the bar to her *nipples*, nearly cringing when she made contact. She did not want to be aroused at the gym, but couldn't keep her thoughts from wondering if Hot Shirtless Guy was this suggestive in the bedroom.

"Good. That's good. Now pull harder."

Oh, she wanted to pull harder, but not on the rower. Somehow, her motivation returned, despite the lack of bare skin showing on his torso. The man's approving smile and head nod seemed to set Maddie's will on fire as she hit the highest RPM she'd ever managed on this evil machine.

Figuring he would leave now that his work was done, Maddie gave the rower a few more firm tugs before cooling down once again. She released her feet from the straps and stood, tripping over the rower's frame.

Hot Shirtless Guy caught her, but not before she head-butted his chest. His strong grip on her arms inspired another surge south. Maddie tried to right herself by planting her hands on his pecs. As the strong muscles flexed under her fingers, she jumped back, tripping over the rower again, this time landing flat on her ass.

"You alright?" he asked, stepping around the machine and crouching next to her.

"Fine. Just, well, I stood up too fast, got a little dizzy after all that vigorous rowing." Did she just say vigorous? Maddie wasn't aware that word was even in her vocabulary.

"Let me get you some water. Don't move." Hot Shirtless Guy moved across the room like a man on a mission, filling a paper cup at the water dispenser before moving with the same determination back to Maddie's sprawl. "Drink it slowly," he advised, holding the cup to her lips.

What she wanted to do was toss the water in her face to snap out of this crazy attraction. This man wasn't her type. Maddie was smart, educated, and she was not looking for a man. Even if she was, this one, with all of his glorious muscles and firm skin, would never be interested in a stress-eater who was still twenty-pounds over her ideal weight and didn't know the proper technique on a rowing machine.

But she followed his command again, taking slow slips until the water was finally gone.

"Do you think you can stand?" he asked, still crouching next to her.

"I'm fine, really," she insisted which earned her a smile. The man had dimples that a girl could fall into and never find her way out.

He held out his hand, but instead of grabbing it, Maddie stared at the lines on his calloused palm, wondering what he did to make them so rough and appealing.

"Let me help you up," he offered, snapping her out of a fantasy-infused daze about what those hands might be capable of.

Craving his touch, Maddie gripped his hand and the energy that surged into her pulled her right off the floor. Maybe it was his strength, or maybe both, but it left her unbalanced and falling against his chest again. Her hand was pressed right against where that tattoo decorated his chest and she traced the lines she couldn't see, imagining her fingers caressing the inked skin without the cotton there.

When his muscles flexed beneath her fingers, Maddie realized she was groping him without invitation. "Sorry," she muttered, stepping back and hoping she was flushed enough from the workout that he didn't recognize her burning cheeks as rare and embarrassing blush.

The man continued to smile, a sparking in his eyes as if he knew Maddie was mentally undressing and fondling his very enticing body. She should say something, prove she was intelligent and educated, but the power of speech abandoned her, a crazy and uncontrolled desire possessing her body and rendering her stupid.

"Go ... I need to go," she stuttered, shaking her head at the stupidity of her declaration. "Thanks for showing, um, teaching me proper technique. On the rower," she pointed at the machine in case he forgot what a rower was and locked her jaw closed before humiliating herself further.

"Happy to help," he drawled. "Any time you want me to show you proper technique, just holler."

Maddie couldn't be sure the double entendre was intentional, but her nipples responded with their own silent plea, sending a surge of yes, please straight to her magical place. The arousal had her cringing and she covered it was a smile before scurrying off. Maddie called upon her skills of self-preservation, scurrying off before hid simples and the rest of him did further damage to her muddled brain and needy body.

~~~

Also Available

Puget Sound ~ Alive With Love Series

The Sound of Consequence (April 2013)
The Sound of Betrayal (August 2013)
The Sound of Suspicion (January 2014)
The Sound of Deception (June 2014)
The Sound of Circumstance (December 2015)
The Sound of Reluctance (Coming Soon)

Fighting Back for Love Series

Relay For Love (May 2011)
A Flame Burns Inside (January 2012)
Worth the Fight (Coming in Soon)

Superstitious Brides Series

Marrying for Love (January 2016)
For the Love of Chocolate (February 2016)

Anthologies

Book Boyfriends Cafe *Summer Lovin'* (May 2015)
14 summer romances from USA Today and National Bestselling
authors (includes *Relay For Love*)

Book Boyfriends Cafe Tall, Dark, & Loaded (January 2016)
6 billionaire romances from USA Today and National Bestselling
authors (includes *Marrying for Love*)

Love Notes Country Music-Themed Collection (April 2016)
8 country-music themed novels and novellas from USA Today
and National Bestselling authors (includes *Broken Strings*)

Meet the Author

Big dreamer and certifiable overachiever Susan Ann Wall embraces life at full speed and volume. She's a beer and tea snob, can be bribed with dark chocolate, and the #1 thing on her bucket list is to be the center of a Bon Jovi flash mob.

Susan is a multi-genre author of racy, rule-breaking romance, women's fiction, and erotic fiction (her erotic titles are published as Ann Victor). Her bragging rights include nine books in three different series, three perfect children, adopting two amazing rescue dogs, and a happily ever after that started while serving in the U.S. Army and has spanned two decades (which is crazy since she's not a day over 29).

In her next life, Susan plans to be a 5 foot 10, size 8 rock star married to a chiropractor and will not be terrified of large bridges, spiders, or quiet people (shiver).

Photo by BLC Photography

You can find Susan online at:
www.susanannwall.com
Facebook: Author Susan Ann Wall
Twitter: @susanannwall

www.ingramcontent.com/pod-product-compliance
Lightning Source LLC
Chambersburg PA
CBHW070458130626
46555CB00003B/1064